AN EAGLE BLIND

AN EAGLE BLIND

BROOKE FIELDHOUSE

Copyright © 2024 Brooke Fieldhouse

The moral right of the author has been asserted.

Apart from any fair dealing for the purposes of research or private study, or criticism or review, as permitted under the Copyright, Designs and Patents Act 1988, this publication may only be reproduced, stored or transmitted, in any form or by any means, with the prior permission in writing of the publishers, or in the case of reprographic reproduction in accordance with the terms of licences issued by the Copyright Licensing Agency. Enquiries concerning reproduction outside those terms should be sent to the publishers.

This is a work of fiction. Names, characters, businesses, places, events and incidents are either the products of the author's imagination or used in a fictitious manner. Any resemblance to actual persons, living or dead, or actual events is purely coincidental.

Troubador Publishing Ltd
Unit E2 Airfield Business Park,
Harrison Road, Market Harborough,
Leicestershire. LE16 7UL
Tel: 0116 2792299
Email: books@troubador.co.uk
Web: www.troubador.co.uk

ISBN 978 1805145 134

British Library Cataloguing in Publication Data.
A catalogue record for this book is available from the British Library.

Printed and bound by CPI Group (UK) Ltd, Croydon, CR0 4YY
Typeset in 12pt Adobe Garamond Pro by Troubador Publishing Ltd, Leicester, UK

ACKNOWLEDGEMENTS

The front epigraph image is a digitally enhanced photograph taken at a location in the UK by the author. Thanks to Troubador Publishing for production and an appropriately mysterious cover design.

*"Everything we see hides another thing.
We always want to see what is hidden by what we see."*
René Magritte

PRELUDE

'Who d'you reckon is going to win? Karpov or Kasparov?'

The voices the young woman can hear are mostly male and in high spirits. *Who cares?* she thinks. *This is a drama students' liberal studies country jaunt, not a chess nerd's convention. Pyjama people, get them out of my way!*

There's the scrape of boots on tarmac, the bump and bounce of other bodies, well upholstered against the early November bite. Bumping because it's cold, but mainly because it's well past closing time at the public house where they've all spent the evening, and which is now a mile behind them.

There's that smell and taste which is the inevitable seasonal decay of leaf and twig, the resonance of garden bonfires, and which at that very moment is overlaid with a more urgent reek of expired saltpetre and Chinese snow. Some of the young men have left the group to let off fireworks, and in that unearthly light which fleetingly remains after a rocket has streaked up past smudgy horizon to sparkle in an ink-perfect sky, the young woman can see emboldened a stone pyramid, the warning finger of an obelisk and, beyond that, the silhouette of a dome.

It's rough grass instead of tarmac under her feet now, and she can no longer feel the press of other bodies. *Something* has made her leave the throng. It was the stentorian call of one of the men, the one whose face is aglow as he clicks down on his cigarette lighter. In his hand is the empty wine bottle, which moments ago he was waving round his head, which he's now using as a rocket launcher. There's another girl standing close to him.

'Cop hold of this, Stace!'

There are three of them – two women, one man. The bitter smell and taste of the air is almost overwhelming the young woman.

The group on the tarmac path is distant now, but the young woman can see a fourth figure. It's another man who's approaching. As the second man reaches her, there is a burst of sparks and all four faces are illuminated as a rocket hurls out its fiery payload. But the rocket is not travelling vertically; it's horizontal.

The voice of the first man is abusive. The second man tears at his clothes, trying to rip off a bomber jacket and scarf. Shockingly, it's impossible to tell screams coming from the rocket and those which are coming out of the second man's mouth. He's stamping, hitting at his thorax, neck, and head, his arms are flailing as if in an act of incomprehensible semaphore. He's become a human Catherine wheel, whose epicentre – where the scorching missile has buried itself in the folds of his scarf – is an iridescence of heliotrope. The young woman hears herself coughing uncontrollably.

'That'll fucking teach you!'

The young man is running on the spot; his hopping body performs a half turn and falls like a felled tree, sparks spewing between his frame and the damp grass. A crackling sound complemented by a burst of fairy pink, ogre's gold and goblin green light turns space between man and ground into the spectre of some infernal grotto. There's a deafening explosion followed by silence, except for a whining; the kind of miserable sound a dog makes after it's just been hit by a motor vehicle. There's a smell of something other than consumed saltpetre.

The young woman can hear people coming back from the pathway. Figures approaching, barely visible through a gauze of grubby white smoke. A young man takes off his leather jacket, wraps it around his hands, and raises the fallen boy's body to kick away the charred debris. The first man has dropped his wine bottle but doesn't come to help.

It's nearly twenty years since it was thought fashionable for young people to wear army surplus greatcoats, but one young man is so dressed and removes it to make a hammock in which to carry the injured man to the house, the student's home for the night. There's groaning coming from the human on the makeshift stretcher.

The group passes the stone obelisk and processes down the slope to the house. The greatcoat hammock is swaying, its contents still moaning. Different members of the procession take it in turns to carry an arm or skirt of the greatcoat. It's like witnessing a prehistoric wake – except the deceased isn't deceased, yet. The young woman can see the lights of the house, the brightest at its main entrance. As the group changes pace to crunch over the gravel forecourt, a voice rasps for water, the sound echoing round the enormous three-sided space. Three men break away from the group and race up the stone steps, the first of the trio wrenching open the glass-panelled door.

By the time the hammock bearers are laying their load at the foot of the steps, the three men are pelting back down, two of them carrying a stretcher which they place next to the hammock. Behind them bustles a woman dressed as an eighteenth-century maid, carrying blanket and jug and followed by two men wearing leather aprons. The "maid" tells the group that an ambulance is on its way, and they manoeuvre the victim onto the stretcher, cover him loosely with the blanket, and wait. Nobody seems to know what to do next.

As if it has spontaneously fallen into prayer, the group is silent. A hiatus whose duration is impossible to gauge is broken by the breathy engine of a large motor vehicle, and faces are spotlit in rapid succession by powerful headlights.

The nostalgic smell of bonfires and – what must now be to most senses – the terrible stench of discharged fireworks has been replaced with a damp mossy air blowing up from the lake. While from a basement window comes no more than a trace of the roast lamb supper which many of the students had enjoyed long before the evening was ruined.

It had been an accident, of course.

THE EVENTS AT GOLIGHTLY

1

Golightly: 2.5 miles nearest village, 12.5 miles nearest working railway station, 25 miles nearest town, 50 miles nearest airport. As she sat in the back of the taxi, Lorna had to admit to herself that she hadn't considered even these basics. What had clinched her choice of creative writing course had been its consistent five-star reviews. Chas had been all for it, revealed that Golightly had world status as a nature reserve, said he'd have given his eye teeth to be the journalist who'd broken the story of the discovery of the *Cortinarius* Golightly mushroom which had been found on the estate ten years ago.

There were other courses being held at Golightly: transcendental meditation, mindfulness and assertiveness, so Lorna would meet a variety of people. She had absolutely no aspirations to be a writer, but this was the course she'd dreamed of. Thirty years as a marketing executive, she'd climbed to the top of her career, to its peak, then retired – just like that.

There were those who'd said she should have stayed. She'd won awards. Brand impact and content marketing had been her specialisms. But she didn't *own* the company – oh, she had shares, but it wasn't *her* creation, wasn't her "baby". She'd ended up with a massive pension pot, and now she was going to explore a different facet of her personality, the part which she had kept hidden all her adult working life. Perhaps even her entire conscious life.

Lorna put her hands on the plaid rug (always to be found on the back seat of a northern minicab) to try and stop herself from moving from side to side. She could feel the tug and sizzle of static as the vehicle swayed and bounced, could sense the ersatz of the air freshener as she watched the dangling Elvis figurine, craftily pivoted to swivel at the hips. The driver, she'd decided, had the domed forehead and gap teeth more akin to those of Elton John.

She could have driven there – to Golightly. Most of the other students would, but she wanted a change. Chas would pick her up at Stevenage on the way back if need be. He'd offered to drive her the whole way, no doubt hoping for a glimpse of an early willow warbler or to hear the zizz of the shrill carder bee, bless him! Chas ought to know about retreats – he knew enough about wildlife reserves.

A vibration came from her bag: a text from Matt, her real baby. Her *only* baby – nothing to do with Chas. *Enjoy the course!* When Matt and Rachel went to live in Brisbane, Lorna had panicked like she'd never done before in her life. But it was okay; they texted, skyped, emailed, and there was always that feeling of everything being at arm's length. Lorna had discovered she liked arm's length.

The drive from station to house was almost ceremonial. Once you'd left the highway, the road went straight; it didn't follow the contours of the geography. There were no fences, no hedges, and no dry-stone walls, something which Lorna had always associated with this part of the country. Twice the driver had to brake in order to squeeze through narrow gatehouses in lines of fortifications. As he did so, Lorna could see the texture of the stone: yellowish, sugary-looking with slitty windows and obviously mock. Anybody could see they'd never defended anything. It was fake, fairy tale, and could have been made out of cough candy. For a moment she wished the window was open so she could have reached her arm through, touched it, tasted it. Finger against tongue, that flavour of clove and aniseed. *Sheer fantasy! Though perhaps not all fantasy, perhaps there was just a frisson of real danger here.*

She'd signed up for the spring course – only two a year, that and autumn. Summer was out because that was when the house got most of its visitors, but the clocks had gone forward so there was a semblance of entering into a new season, and she didn't know this part of the country. Such a far cry from Matching Thorpe!

"Elton John", it appeared, was operating an unofficial shuttle service from the railway station. He wanted to know where Lorna was from, which course, and whether she'd been on one before. He had already acquired the profiles of other students.

'Abigail, she's from Connecticut, Debbie from Devon, and Manic, he's from Punjab… of course,' he added, just in case Lorna should be in any doubt about his ethnic origin.

Five o'clock, so she'd be too late for afternoon tea. It was gusty outside; she'd noticed *that* as soon as she'd got off the train. *Golightly: 550 feet elevation above sea level.* There were grubby purple clouds moving at high-speed and leaving a ragged edge between earth and sky. An edge which had a quality, as if dabbed at by some chiaroscuro painter, and it was beneath the brightest of that impasto which Lorna caught sight of a stone pyramid. And before that dim recollection had the chance to wither, the taxi slowed, and directly ahead was the dark bulk of an obelisk tapering into the even darker sky.

'This is it!' Elton nodded. And there it was, the gilded dome of Golightly, and as the car drew up to the foot of the wide stone steps leading up to the main entrance, Lorna wished that – spectacular as it seemed – she had done a little more research before choosing the location for her course.

'You might just make it for tea,' said Elton.

2

As the taxi scratched its way back across the gravel forecourt and ploughed round the corner of the west wing, Lorna felt a wave of melancholy break over her. No offer to help her up the steps with her wheeled luggage. In a hurry, but for what? She was almost certainly the last to arrive. There was nothing round here. This was the back of beyond.

For one moment she was tempted to take out her phone and call him – or one of his colleagues – and get the hell out of there. Then she remembered there was no signal. The course information had made that clear.

Matt's text had got through in the nick of time. *After all, it is a retreat, Lorna!*

And why, precisely, *was* she here? Answer: to start living the creative life! After a career of being "brilliant", she could afford to experiment a little. And why exactly are *we* here? *I mean people, mankind, Lorna.* Answer: to find our unique creativity, and develop it, of course! How many people have the freedom to do that?

'How many careers do people have in their lives?' Chas had said. 'Some don't even have *one*. Out of the world population of 7.8 billion, only 3.4 billion of them are employed, Lorna. And only a tiny proportion of those will actually have a career. You couldn't have been more of a success, so everything which happens now is a bonus!'

She'd seen so many in the world of commerce; aspiring, achieving and acquiring the trappings: the boutique apartments, the villa in La Gomera, the high-performance cars, and – until lockdown – the relentless world travel. She'd observed them, growing old yet insisting that they were part of the "forever young brigade". She'd seen them skimming over the surface of life – as she herself had done – and as old age closed in and beckoned to them to look under, to dig deeper before it was too late, she'd seen them fail to answer the call, and finally she watched them flop. *She* was going to dare to follow her intuition, and to expand her powers of invention.

But that was her bravado of yesterday; today she was apprehensive. Scared of failing, and she was frightened of something else she might find here. Just exactly what, she wasn't sure. Carrying only her shoulder bag, she walked slowly up the pale and worn stone stairway. It was long, no ramps, and the handrail wasn't really a handrail, it was a lumpy stone balustrade, and the stair was so wide she couldn't reach any handrail anyway. *What if they had wheelchairs? But they had sedan chairs then, didn't they? People were carried, not always the agile bearing the lame, it was the poor lifting the rich.* She paused to open the glass-panelled door, but it opened silently, seemingly of its own accord. Yet there was no one there, so she stepped over the threshold and into the Great Hall.

Lovely! A scent of freesias, her favourite. But what tiny flowers for such a huge space! And no sign of the actual plants; everything here was made from marble and paint. It was a Herculean stage set made solid. Space layered upon space. Where there were spaces, you could look beyond into the next space, and where it was solid, the artists had created the effect of yet more space. The scenes on the walls depicted: earth, air, fire and water; Mercury, Neptune and Apollo; and there were maenads – the women of Bacchus. It was a restless and relentless montage of elements and gods. Breathtaking! Yet somehow Lorna couldn't help feeling that today the epicurean feelings stirred by these images were intended for others and not her.

'Elaine Wayfarer; day reception!'

Yes, Lorna remembered the emails, but she hadn't expected such adumbrations of 1940s glamour. Oh, this was an ordinary enough-looking face. But the grey wool suit, cream silk shirt, black stockings – no doubt matching suspender belt embracing slim hips under the three-quarter length skirt – black patent shoes, and red lips! The hair was authentic 1948; BBC TV make-up couldn't have done better. It made Lorna's white chinos, brown loafers, pale blue cambric shirt and neck-tie scarf worn under a hacking jacket, and mousy pixie cut look perhaps appropriate for travel – expensive, even – but unoriginal. No handshake, not in the age of anno virus, but, thank God, no mask. That would have kiboshed the image well and truly.

'You must be Lorna.'

She had to be and, as the words were spoken, Lorna was conscious of an almost imperceptible whisper of chatter coming from the nether layers of the giant space in which she and the svelte female were standing. There was, behind the freesias, just a faint whiff of whatever it might be for supper.

'You're not too late for tea.'

'It's okay, I'll give it a miss.' She'd done it deliberately.

Perfectly choreographed but entering from a different part of the stage was a dour figure. Male, jowly, head an ash-grey suede bullet, and clad in grey shirt and trousers covered with a long, brown leather apron.

'Blogg will take your luggage up.'

Blogg? How hilariously gothic! But even as Lorna smiled, she remembered her luggage and turned to look through the glass doors. There was something desperately uncomfortable about the way she had left it abandoned on the gravel at the foot of the grand steps which made her predicament seem almost unbearable. She hesitated, took the white A4-size folder from Elaine's outstretched hand.

'The course details...' And after what seemed an even longer pause, 'And the student list – just *your* course, not the others; everybody wears labels. We couldn't release it to you before, for obvious reasons.'

For a split-second, Lorna wondered... *Of course! Security. Now she was here, no internet, so no looking people up.* Under normal circumstances, Lorna looked everybody up; most people did. That was the point of the internet – communication, foreknowledge and basic marketing currency.

Lorna opened the folder. Nervously she scanned the names:

Abigail Gritsch
Boone Fockler
Debbie Hosmer
Drew Hedgepath
Jenna Haste
Juliet Goosen
Lorna Collins
Manic Phut
Nina Tallent
Nisi von Waggoner
Traci Mushens
Trish Westfall

No familiar names. She glanced up and, as if in a surrealistic dream, could see Elaine's crimson lips balanced on the edge of what might be a pool of amusement. *Obviously an established ritual. Those on the list would all be "high achievers"; the course price tag was astronomical. Only three men* – nobody she knew, but just for good measure she checked the eight other women, concentrating on first names only this time. Lorna exhaled slowly – and invisibly, she hoped.

'Supper is in the dining room at 6.30. There's a seating layout – you're all in course groups. There'll be an opportunity to mix with the other students in the breakout before the evening course introductions. Enjoy!'

Elaine remained where she was as – again with exquisite timing – a third figure tapped its way onto the colossal stage set. This time it was female; young, dressed in a white bonnet, a matching apron worn over a long black skirt. There was a low-cut neck under which was a high-collared yellow blouse. Lorna was sure that Elaine could see how impressed she was with the whole presentation.

'This is Betty; she'll show you to your room.'

Like a silent shadow, her loafers noiseless on the marble steps, Lorna followed Betty up one of two grand staircases. Under flower-encrusted, fat Corinthian columns they climbed, past swags and garlands rendered in stone and plaster, beneath multiple gods: Zeus, Hera, Iris and Athena. The steady tap of Betty's house shoes – dun-coloured, Lorna couldn't help noticing as Betty gathered up her skirts to mount the steps. Already, there seemed to be a conscious delineation of dress in the world of Golightly; eighteenth century for house menials, 1940s for middle management.

'You're in the servants' quarters; two floors up, I'm afraid.'

'No need to be afraid on either count, Betty.'

The course literature had emphasised the importance of "bonding", perhaps implying that might extend to fun in "the dorm". *No, thank you! There would be a snorer who you have to face the next morning and be nice to while all along building up an intense hatred for them.*

'Given the choice of sleeping communally, braving the sound of sawing logs, I opted for the guarantee of a good night's sleep – solo!'

"Betty", judging from her received pronunciation, was probably a college intern, quite likely ex-private school and almost certainly not called Betty but perhaps Tory, or maybe even Annunziata. Early adulthood for Lorna had been Harlow new town – Mum and Dad had been given a choice when they were rehoused from Dagenham: Basildon or Harlow. Mum thought Harlow was posher because it seemed like country.

Betty was tap-tapping lightly now over the polished wood block floors of landing and passage, and as Lorna followed Betty's bobbing white bonnet, the corridor looked endless. They passed giant ormolu-framed mirrors, bow and serpentine-fronted tables on which stood huge bowls of Chinese-looking origin. On one side there were windows through which Lorna caught glimpses of a large lake. On the other side there were doors. Doors so big, they looked as if they had been made for humans who were twice normal size. *But weren't people smaller then?* They looked even grander with their panelled wood surrounds and pointy bits on top. One of the doors was ajar, and Lorna could see into a room, large and full of early evening light. There were six beds and two young women were sitting on one of the beds talking. It looked cosy.

'You could have been in that room if you'd wanted.'

Lorna was standing staring, not wistfully or anything; she was simply gripped by a feeling that she *had already* slept in that room. Then, there had been many beds in it. Then, there had been no mirrors, no ornate tables or Chinese bowls. Then, at the end of the corridor there had been boys' bedrooms. *Those boys!* So much hijinks – all the beds had been on wheels… Then, something happened to change everything… It was gone – the memory, that was.

Memory can be a little like a live animal, reluctant to be brought into the light and put under scrutiny, but Lorna had been increasingly aware of that fact all through her life.

'Are you alright?' Lorna saw Betty check herself. Lorna must have given her an angry look, so she smiled at her just in case Betty was feeling she'd stepped out of line by questioning Lorna's health. *What she should have said was, "Is everything alright?" – like a concerned maître d'. It's not her fault, she just needs more training. That's the thing about the middle classes, they don't know anything about training, just like they don't know anything about hygiene and cleaning.*

'It seemed familiar in there.'

'You're not the first person to say that.'

That was a relief. It wasn't just *her* getting the vibe. It wasn't as if Lorna hadn't travelled the world or anything. She'd visited big country houses before, been to the European Baroque palaces of Schleissheim and Nymphenburg, but there was something right here that was bewitching her. Golightly certainly was amazing, and you couldn't deny that it was bound to awaken all sorts of sensations. They didn't *need* to have happened before.

Without warning, Betty made an abrupt turn to the left and stopped. They were in a dark wood-panelled circular lobby adjacent to the corridor they had just left. Ahead was yet another seemingly endless corridor, except this time Lorna noticed there were no windows, just doors on either side, and between each door, curvy golden lamp brackets with glass bowls spilling a pale-yellow light. It was an almost mesmerising composition of converging parallels. The lobby wall had been *pochéd* or hollowed out. Two pockets on either side which contained more Chinese stuff – figurines this time. Between each of the pairs of recesses was a door, slightly curved to follow the form of the wall. But the doors had no frames or architraves; they were almost invisible except for the handle – *a modern addition,* thought Lorna. *That was why; servants were meant to be invisible – even when they were needed.*

'Almost there!' Betty pulled the outward-opening door and stepped inside into what seemed to be a kind of miniaturised netherworld of a narrow upward-leading staircase and low ceiling. Betty's ballet pump-style footwear touched the sides of the stair. Clonk! It was wood, hollow, a more recent carpet runner in the centre, and walls panelled to waist height and painted a "tasteful" but rather dead heritage green. The wall above dado height appeared to have been misted in some whey-coloured substance.

At the top of the stairs was a short length of corridor, three doors on either side, and at the end of which, through an open door, Lorna could see sunlight falling upon a claw-footed bath.

'The bathroom's shared, but don't worry, the bedrooms aren't all occupied. Most students opted for the communal choice of the old state rooms on the floor below. You've only got one neighbour. This is where most of the servants would have slept; women on this side of that lobby, men on the other. The difference is that you get the room to yourself; three hundred years ago, it would have been three or even five to a room!'

Betty opened the door. It was lovely, *sort of Shaker* and just what she'd had in mind. The only thing was, there was no lock on the door.

3

Lorna closed the door behind her. *Stupid! What must that intern have thought?* She sat on the bed. There *was* no memory. She had *not* been here before. There was her wheeled luggage, laid on the leather cradle in front of the window and, my word, look at that view!

It was evening but not yet dusk, and the dark clouds which had accompanied her arrival had been replaced with clear – if cold-looking – blue sky. Low sun, long shadows, and a landscape little changed since 1740. She could see a fountain playing in the centre of the lake. *Funny, just for the benefit of the fifty or so students. There would be no public visitors this week. Perhaps they were testing it after the winter.* She wondered how it was switched on and off. Chas had said it was fed by water falling from the hill behind the house where there was a reservoir.

She opened the A4 folder again; on the left, a pouch containing her label: *Lorna Collins, Creative Writing*. On the right, the list she'd already scrutinised and, beyond that, an itinerary:

- *Creative writing*
- *Transcendental Meditation*
- *Assertiveness*
- *Mindfulness*

Timetable as follows:

Day 1

4.00 – arrive (not before if possible), tea and biscuits available in the breakout area
6.30 – supper in the dining room
7.15 – introduction by Golightly
7.30 – tea/coffee and general mingle in the breakout area
8.00 – retire into course groups for introductory chats, personal introductions
9.30 – rest of evening free, bar available for those who wish
10.00 – curfew

Day 2

8.00 – breakfast in the dining room
10.00 – group classes
11.15 – break
11.30 – group classes
12.45 – lunch in the dining room
2.00 – group classes
3.15 – break
3.30 – group classes
4.45 – own time
6.00 – supper in the dining room
6.45 – tea/coffee and general mingle in the 'breakout' area
7.15 – talk or presentation in course groups
9.00 – rest of evening free, bar available for those who wish
10.00 – curfew

Days 3 to 5 to follow the same form.

Day 6
8.00 – breakfast in the dining room
10.00 – goodbyes
Please be away by 11.15

There were a further two things troubling Lorna. The 7.15 introduction made it sound as if the house itself would be speaking, and what was all this curfew business?

4

'Just through there!' Elaine Wayfarer had nodded in the direction of the weird whisper which had been "tea", and which Lorna had decided to give a miss. Here now and standing in the Great Hall just a touch after 6.30, she could once again hear the buzz. But where was it actually coming from? It seemed to be emanating from one of the great staircases itself.

Lorna had imagined students would be dining in one of the formal areas, but just as she was sleeping in what would have been servants' quarters, it made sense that they were all going to be eating below stairs. She peered round the back of the staircase; the buzz rose to a clamour, the toothsome odour stronger. There was a stair leading down, marble, as were the walls, but at its foot the grandeur of the entrance hall above was stripped away to reveal a simple stone floor and roughcast walls – the working territory of servants from a bygone age. There were no plaster frolicking cherubs or grape-squeezing satyrs down here. A metal wall sconce with live flame endowed the scene with a twitching sense of movement. Lorna was late again.

Late because, quite frankly, she'd fallen asleep. After examining the student list for a third time and satisfying herself that there were no familiar names, the relief was so intense that she'd stretched out, head on pillow, and the next thing she knew it was 6.15. A freshen up would have to do, so would the chinos. She'd substituted the cambric shirt for a silk kimono jacket. She wasn't on a bloody cruise; it was hardly going to be the captain's table.

As Lorna reached the end of the corridor and walked through a wide opening in the stone wall, the clamour rose to a din. The space in which she found herself was long, low and dark, but stabbed with hundreds of tiny moving lights. Candles! Two big circles of them on each of the four oversized tables, three tiers high, and reaching almost to the vaulted roof. Everything seemed to be moving, the vast room a landscape of shadow which seemed to advance and recede. She searched for the seating plan, but all she could see was a pale hand waving frantically to and fro. Beneath it a figure, standing tall, female, brunette-bobbed, and wearing a dark evening dress.

'You're *here*!' The younger woman was mouthing because of the general roar and pointing at the chair next to hers. 'I'm so glad; we thought you weren't coming.'

Lorna abruptly sat down as directed.

'You must be Lorna Collins,' the tall one mouthed once more while resuming her own seat. Lorna, no label – she'd left it in her room; *Juliet Goosen* said the lady's.

Lorna's chair was at the side end of a table for twelve – five-a-side plus one at each end, Juliet at the end. On Lorna's other side was Manic Phut. She smiled, he smiled. The racket was so intense, that was all it seemed that they could do.

She'd been wrong about the dress code. There was more than a sprinkling of bow ties, not on *her* table where there were only three men, but on the three tables beyond. All forty-eight students were seated at abnormally wide, dark wooden tables. There was no crisp table linen, only mats which seemed to be made from a substance resembling black rubber, and Lorna ran the back of her finger across its ribbed surface. It felt curiously comforting.

The worst thing was the noise which seemed to be coming from above their heads. The room was a windowless cellar, a dungeon, its vaulted stone ceiling no higher than an arm's length above the shoulders of the tallest men. Above each of the tables was an opening in the ceiling the width of the tabletop. Its internal edges were stepped as if it were the bottom of a chimney. Lorna peered up it, expecting to see the light of an oculus, but all she could see was black space. A man opposite was standing, reaching into its depths, perhaps trying to investigate the source of the sound. In the scintillating light, Lorna couldn't read his label as he stretched his arm above his head.

'Boom!' Juliet seemed to be saying, pointing in the direction of the mysterious black shaft.

Lorna thought that the sound was more of a hiss than a boom, like white noise.

'Boom!' Juliet mouthed again; this time she had produced her white folder, open at the course members list, and she was pointing at the name Boone Fockler. Of course, they'd met at teatime so all had had a chance to get to know a bit about one another. All to the good because, as things stood, the present ambience wasn't exactly going to be conducive to mutual soul-searching.

It seemed that mime was the only possible form of human communication. Juliet's hand covering her ear, her finger pointing at Boone. Boone's chin nodding to Juliet, his hand inside the giant chimney as if it was groping to find the fan switch on the kitchen cooker vent, except here everything was scaled up to Orson Welles proportions.

Boone's shoulders shrugged, his finger flicking beyond the table, and Lorna noticed that the cellar had become populated with "Bettys". Eight young women dressed identically to Betty were moving between the four tables carrying water jugs, baskets containing what looked like bread rolls, and periodically pausing to wipe an unimaginably imperfect glass tumbler or an item of cutlery. All – in addition to their Betty outfits – were wearing white disposable face masks. Two further masked Bettys were standing at waiter stations, while in the distance beyond the shimmering upland of candelabra, Lorna could just make out Boone's inclined head encased in a vignette with Elaine Wayfarer's upturned face, her glossed lips this time hidden behind a pale grey mask. Boone, too, seemed to have acquired a face covering.

Boone loped back into full view, sat down, and took out his A4 folder. He flourished a whiteboard marker, which Lorna noticed formed part of each person's place setting, and – remaining masked even though seated – proceeded to write something using more than one sheet of paper. He got to his feet and, in the style of Bob Dylan's presentation of *Subterranean Homesick Blues*, held up the folder for the rest of the table to see. *Sensory*, read the first sheet, which he let flutter to the tabletop. *Deprivation*, indicated the second, which he also let fall from his hand. *Is part of*, informed the third page, which, with a show of finality, he tore away and let drop to the floor to reveal, *The experience*. With that, he removed his mask and sat down. There was no shocked silence, just an infuriating hiss.

The food began arriving. Everything was in nouvelle cuisine quantities and delivered in white bowls, each no more than four inches in diameter. There'd been no menu, apparently no choice. Then Lorna remembered the forms she'd had to fill in online. They'd been numerous, the questions comprehensive: *vegan, gluten-free, dairy*. Whether you were taking vitamin or Q10 supplements. There'd even been questions on oxalates and uric acid. It seemed that each person's meal was bespoke, and the dishes kept coming, the Bettys in constant motion between table and wherever the kitchens were.

There were lots of green shoots, which looked like samphire, and hummus-like dips, some cold, others hot, some spicy, others not. Lorna hadn't a clue what she was eating but it was delicious. Neither, apparently, had Juliet; the two of them were managing to communicate in their own way, heads together and, perhaps because of the strangeness of the situation, becoming increasingly frivolous.

Lorna thought she had better try and communicate with Manic because the person on his other side wasn't. She'd once attended a conference in Chandigarh so felt confident enough to try her luck.

'The Punjab?'

Manic paused mid-samphire, eyebrows raised. He took out his white folder, reached for the board marker, which was lying next to his dessert spoon, and wrote – with some indignation, thought Lorna – *Sarajevo*.

Dishes continued to arrive, delivered with the efficiency of a territorial army and in such profusion that it was impossible to gauge the passing of time. When no further bowls had come, all empty ones had been removed, and everybody had stopped eating, what came over Lorna was a sensation that, as if at one stroke, someone had changed the entire air supply within the room. It was a resonance, and so deep at first as to register as a boom. It grew into a more insistent bonging, then a ding, a multiple chime, until it felt as if each of the forty-eight seated humans was engaged in sounding his own carillon. And rather like the experience of having been held within a physical grip for a long period, and which had been suddenly released, the hiss was no more.

As the last chime melted, there was total silence within the room, except for the tinkle of teaspoons. Not only did it feel like there had been a change of air, but the whole room seemed to alter in scale. The walls appeared nearer, people bigger, and everything looked more colourful.

Lorna hadn't noticed it before, but at the end of the chamber, its floor was raised to form a narrow stage. Standing on the stone floor in front of the stage was the source of the sound. Tubular bells. They were glinting, swaying busily in the candlelight, and at either end of the metal frame of hanging bells, Lorna could see the crisp, laundered whiteness of chefs torques. Two figures stood dressed in double-breasted white coats and matching aprons. Each had identical waxed moustaches and Charles I style whiskers. The masked Bettys circulated the tables, pouring teas and coffees, while the two chefs remained motionless like sentries.

Without warning, from behind what looked like Italian painted screens at each side of the stage darted two small, grinning figures. They ran towards one another, crossing in the centre. *Children?* And like Blogg, they were dressed in leather – but this time miniature – aprons. Both carried flambeaux which they thrust up to iron sconces mounted on the wall, and bursts of flame illuminated the stage as the figures vanished behind the screens. Out of the gloom of a niched recess, into the live light stepped a tall figure.

'I…' There was a calculated pause. 'Am Golightly, your host for the duration. *Welcome!*'

'Sooo hammy!' whispered Juliet.

It was true. Immaculate grey suit – again with a 1940s older English tailored cut. Trousers of a wider variety, and high-rise. Jacket with hand-stitched lapels, double-breasted and fitting perfectly the etiolated limbs of what looked like an elderly silver-haired gent. His head was of the kind where one's attention is immediately drawn to the prominence of the skull, and the size and position of its scissor teeth. As he spoke, he rocked backwards, then forwards, while pushing up with his toes to emphasise his already impressive height. He was performing as if his audience was one collective body that he was going to take a bite out of.

Lorna wasn't sure if it was the effect of the naked flame on the sides of his head or whether there really was something of the undead about him. It was as if the person had once been suave, but all the life had gradually leaked out of him. *The guilt of self-abuse – that's it! A life enslaved by intensive masturbation. The eyes never resting yet glazed. The sockets bruised, and the cheeks cadaverous.* It seemed obvious to Lorna that there had never been a Lady Golightly.

'Firstly, our thanks to the Van Dyck brothers. Not only for the melodiousness of their peal – or should I say, their *ap*peal.'

There were arpeggios of laughter, counterpointed with the chink of coffee cups.

'As you are now aware, not only do they create meals of great flavour, texture and depth, they are also talented musicians.'

Both brothers bowed solemnly and simultaneously, like mechanical bookends. Enthusiastic applause from the diners, and the duo removed itself, walking abreast and disappearing through the double doorway next to the stage, their starched white torques only just clearing the door head.

Lorna could see that all eight Bettys had meanwhile assembled in a line in front of the stage, directly below the gaunt figure of Golightly.

'We thank also those who have prepared and served.'

More applause and the Bettys curtseyed in unison, taking short delicate steps in their ballet pumps and following in the wake of the two chefs.

'But their labours – as far as evening meals go – for the week are at an end…' Another pause. 'For the next four evenings, *you…*' – Golightly's skeletal arms suddenly extended and made a grand chopping motion, as if he had in an instant condemned all forty-eight students to some fearful fate – 'will be doing the cooking, serving, and washing up.'

There was a roar of laughter, a flurry of open mouths, a wave of raised eyebrows, even stamping on the floor and banging on the oak board in a "get away!" exclamation of disbelief. There were also smiles from those who knew and were enjoying seeing the reaction from those who didn't.

'There's nothing to fear; you will be working in your groups of twelve – how you organise yourselves will be part of the experience. You will be given *raw* materials…'

Lorna fancied that Golightly was relishing an emphasis on the word "raw", as if he'd really wanted to say "excoriated".

'… A set of instructions, but most of all you will have at your disposal – but *only* if you must – the expert advice of the Van Dycks. They are *not* there to do it for you, only to offer verbal advice. The team which sets, clears, and washes up will be the team which prepares, cooks and serves the following evening. Oh, and there's no *need* for you to dress up in eighteenth-century costume, that's optional.'

There was further laughter, but this time rather lacking gusto.

'It's not a competition, just enjoy! I won't bore you with the history of the house. You'll perhaps discover *that* over the course of the week. If you have any time, that is!'

More laughter, thinly spread.

'Just before I hand over to our business manager extraordinaire – or should I perhaps say, *formida-a-able*…' – a few further stout-hearted chuckles from the tables at Golightly's Rococo pronunciation – 'Sir John Spreighmont…'

Somehow, during the meal, Lorna and Juliet had

managed to communicate sufficiently to discover that not only had they both originated from Dagenham but had also been to the same school – not at the same time; Juliet must have been fifteen years younger. This, together with the outlandishness of the evening, had combined to produce in them a state of mutual giggliness.

'Sounds like an over-territorial randy tomcat,' Juliet whispered. The name *had* appeared in the correspondence, and in print gave off perhaps a hint of equestrian grandeur, but coming from the lips of Golightly, it made both women want to chuckle.

'…Who will explain the rules of the house. There's one last thing I'd like to stress. This is a *retreat*. The word contains a special meaning which I'm sure you all appreciate. You're not prisoners here.'

Uncertain laughter.

'We're not forcing you to do anything. The emphasis is on trust,' – momentary pause – '*mutual trust*!' This was delivered so unexpectedly loudly that eyes blinked, hands twitched, and coffee cups rattled. 'You've demonstrated *your* trust in us by paying the not exactly trifling fee.'

Laughter – a little more fulsome this time.

'I sincerely hope that *we* can trust you?' His tone was almost beseeching. 'I thank you all.' With that, Golightly abruptly turned and walked out of sight behind one of the Italian screens. There were perfunctory explosions of hand upon hand, a variety of incomprehensible expressions, and Lorna had the sudden idea that whatever system might be employed to heat this cellar had, for some reason, been abruptly switched off.

Before the buzz of chatter could resume, a second figure, this time dark-haired and moustachioed, stepped forward from the niche into the pulsing light and stood without speaking but as if waiting for a cue. The man possessed a similar 1940s buttoned-down, hand-stitched look, and, perhaps seized by the drama, for one incredulous moment Lorna thought it was Matt – her own son. Matt didn't have a moustache, but it was the way the man was standing, the line of his jaw, his mouth – though so much harder than Matt's – and there was something about his ears. The feeling was so strong that in a reassurance-seeking instant she wanted to reach out and touch Juliet's hand. Then it was gone; the man must have been twenty years older than Matt.

He prattled on in monotone about fire regulations: no-smoking rules, no wi-fi, no visitors, use of the office telephone, and how students must *not* charge their phones in their rooms but hand them in to the office before supper where they would be charged and returned after the evening individual course sessions. Everything about the man was quick-fire, punctuated with glances at his wristwatch. Lorna was glad she had not reached for Juliet.

'More upmarket porn film, I'd say,' whispered Juliet, with a slight snort.

'If you have something to say, we'd like you to share it. We take a dim view of secrets here.'

It was so quick that Lorna didn't take in what

Spreighmont had said until she realised the man's eyes were on her, *her*, not Juliet.

He continued. 'As Lord Golightly has said, you're not prisoners here; the front door will be left open and night staff will be on duty, but we ask you all to observe a ten o'clock curfew.' He paused before adding breathily and sotto voce, 'It's for your own good.'

There was polite and rather flimsy laughter which petered out almost straight away.

'Any questions?' he barked, again looking straight at Lorna.

'I have to Skype with my ten-year-old on Thursday. It's his birthday,' from a bespectacled man sitting on the "assertiveness" table. Juliet had already pointed out which course groups were sitting at which tables.

'No skyping. If you want to have a telephone conversation, come to the office and see me.'

'He'll be mortified!' There was a modicum of camp theatre in the man's protest, but he was serious and disappointed, Lorna could tell.

'It does make it clear in the literature. Next!'

Another hand had shot up, a bluestocking-looking woman on Lorna's table with an American accent.

'I need to tell my three-year-old a bedtime story on Tuesday and Thursday. Lance is doing it this evening, Wednesday, and Friday—'

'Come see me at the office, and I'm pleased to hear you say "tell" rather than "*read*". H'oever *heeyre*!' he bellowed in the style of a circus ringmaster, his hand slicing horizontally through the air.

It was a small woman with a round face, tubular-shaped upper body, and a pouchy look around the eyes, sitting on the "mindfulness" table: 'My parents are renting one of the cottages at Parksfield on the estate...' She was speaking very slowly and with utmost seriousness. Time seemed to slow. The tinkling of porcelain excruciatingly audible. 'I would like to eat with them on Thursday as it's Daddy's birthday, and they would like to come and see my room—'

'We can't prevent you leaving the premises to do the first – you'll miss an evening session, of course – but absolutely *no* to the second!' he yelled back.

Lorna didn't disagree with Spreighmont's answer. This should have been thought about and discussed with those concerned before this evening, but it was his bullying manner which was so horrible. The girl looked as if she was going to burst into tears. Lorna couldn't help it; her hand shot up.

'I'm sure this can be—'

Spreighmont's right hand slapped out through the air in Lorna's direction and made the kind of rapid patting motion an angry parent might make to a child who has just uttered the unsayable. His eyebrows arched and his moustache twitched.

'I'm sorry to interrupt,' she insisted, 'but surely this can be discussed in more depth in private?'

Spreighmont's hand swept back towards the girl. 'If you would, *care* to come see me after breakfast tomorrow morning.'

It seemed that until tomorrow, the matter was closed.

A few curious heads had turned towards Lorna's table. Somebody opposite muttered a "Well interrupted!". For the third time, Lorna could feel the man's eyes on her, and she could feel a fear, an old fear, a remembered fear. She clenched her toes, tried to breathe steadily. She'd been in the wrong about the heckle – except, of course, it hadn't been *her*. But her intervention on the last matter had been decidedly more complex. She'd challenged authority, a peculiar authority. Even if Golightly seemed more like an effete, pussycattish Alistair Sim than the predatorial Nosferatu figure he'd been trying to convey, then *this* person was spot on as a cocky but humourless Groucho Marx in a particularly nasty and abrupt mood. Unarguably an impressive performance and one which perhaps had gone some way to summoning up sympathy for the devil. There was nothing Lorna could do except keep inconspicuous and perhaps learn to distance herself a little from Juliet.

5

'Oh dear! I got you into a bit of trouble, sorrrry.' Juliet didn't exactly sound it, but it was no more than a combination of high spirits from her and bad luck on Lorna's part. 'I can't understand why he picked on you in the first place; he knew it was me who'd heckled. You don't *know* him, do you?'

'Never seen him before.' Lorna wished that she could have spoken with more conviction.

'You were right to stick up for that girl, even though she can't have read the terms of the course contract properly… but I thiiink the poor thing's a wee bit "challenged". I mean, if nobody wants to go rushing to beg permission from his *lordship* at the office, they can always walk up to Cracklewood.'

'What?' Juliet certainly could "rabbit".

'The reservoir; evidently it's the only place near the house where you can get a signal, but it's a bit of climb.'

The breakout room was almost identical to the cellar which they'd just left. Same layout, vaulted roof, and stage at one end. There were two differences: no mysterious chimneys making hissing noises, and instead of rough stone, the walls were panelled in dark oak. There were two seating areas, provided with leather-upholstered Chesterfield sofas, low glass-topped coffee tables, and wall sconces which, although gently flickering, seemed to be electric but dimmed right down. One disconcerting detail was that the wall panels above dado rail height were mirrored, which made a furtive addition to an already secretive subterranean atmosphere. Lorna had once been on a management course held at Cliveden: *Ye-es*, she thought, as she recalled the basement rooms there, *something very Christine Keeler and Stephen Ward about it all!*

The room seemed packed. Hardly anybody was sitting down, though a few were perched on the wide arms of the shiny Chesterfields. Everyone was trying to talk at once. It was as if the dining room had been holding captive its sounds, while in this room there seemed to be a danger of all sound escaping. No doubt *all* were experiencing a feeling of relief to get away from the near hysteria of the last few minutes.

It had been Lorna's intention to chat with students from other courses, but with people wedged together around the giant Chesterfields it was impossible to circulate. Folk seemed in a state of herd agitation after the, quite frankly, unpleasant presentation they'd all just witnessed. On the other side of the nearest Chesterfield island from Lorna was a man with turmeric-coloured hair whose label read, *Ian the Red, Transcendental.* He was leaning over Krisia Banasik, *Mindfulness,* and bellowing.

'Not knowing the time and day of one's death actually makes one immortal!'

'Bianuah Buddhism!' clamoured another voice, as if it were a football chant. Before Lorna could speak to Carla Dawson, *Assertiveness*, who was standing next to her, Bob Brooksbank – also *Assertiveness* – cut in, apparently resuming some yarn about metamorphosis.

'There's this character who reinvents himself, but there's another who literally throws off his husk and is reborn!'

Meanwhile, Brooksbank was being leant upon by a very large woman whose label – apart from the *Assertiveness* bit – had been smudged. She spoke in a high and breathless voice.

'So, you must not trust Bob, because he is in the habit of always giving pleasant answers.'

There was a mystifying pause.

'Looks like you're in for a treat there.' Lorna had actually managed to speak; it was a kind of satirical aside meant just for Carla, who turned and looked at her in a way which made Lorna wish she hadn't spoken at all.

*

Exactly one hour and twenty minutes later, Lorna was back in the same place. This time she was sitting down. She was a little elated, quietly confident, and unlike earlier in the evening, agreeably relaxed. The group session had been everything she might have wanted. The tutors were professional, the group already gelling. The projects would no doubt stretch her without being too daunting. They had even discussed the catering plan. Their group would be cooking on the Friday evening. It would take their minds off the final session which to most would be a challenge, and to some an ordeal.

'You don't *have* to read your work to the rest of the group,' said one of the tutors, 'but I most *strongly* recommend that you do.'

The unpleasantness of the early evening Lorna now attributed to excusable English eccentricity. It was marketing with an ironic twist and she certainly knew *all* about that.

Half the students had retired to their rooms, which meant there was space for all present to sit if they wished, though, as before, some were perched on the arms of the sofas. It meant that if you wanted, you could get six people sitting on one giant seating unit; it made space, created distance so you weren't eavesdropping on another group's chat. The Bettys seemed to have gone home – presumably those who did not live in. Sounds other than talk came from the occasional clink of bottles and glasses as a few students helped themselves from the honesty bar which was located at the stage end of the room. Conversations were hushed, the only other sounds in the room being the soft trilling of the bar's cold cabinet and the occasional squeak of leather as someone adjusted their position on one of the sofas. It seemed that Lorna was not the only person enjoying a feeling of well-being. The only disconcerting thing was the large number of mirrors in the room. Lorna found that when you went up close, she fancied that she could see lights and movement somewhere beyond them.

Lorna had found herself in a Chesterfield corral of six. There was Boone, Juliet, Nisi von Waggoner, and Kerri Krinkler from Mindfulness; it was good they were mixing with other groups. There was also Trish Westfall from her own group, who hadn't said much during the individual introductions, just sat there with a worried look, rather like a little dachshund, so it would be good to find out a bit more about her.

'You know about the zodiac room, don't you?' Kerri apparently had arrived on the dot of 4.00 and had done some exploring. Juliet had heard about – but hadn't actually *seen* – it. 'It's amazing. Circular, domed, and there are all the signs of the zodiac around the walls done in these crazy mosaics… and there's nothing in it, just this patterned marble floor. It's really spooky.'

'We have to see it *now*.' Juliet was talking as if the evening would be incomplete without it. 'Is it open?'

'That's how I'm telling you.'

'We've got twenty minutes before curfew.' Nisi was making it sound like one of those TV challenge shows where you're locked in a room and have to solve a clue in order to get the key and escape.

'Yes, but the curfew is only for going out of the building; this is just upstairs.' Boone sounded keen as well.

'It feels like school – out of bounds and stuff.'

Not like Lorna's school it wasn't. She was beginning to have more doubts about Juliet.

'Come on, Boone! We need a man to lead the way.' Juliet was pulling him from his near horizontal pose on the broad arm of the Chesterfield.

They walked in procession, following Kerri and tapping their way up the marble stair. Evidently, it wasn't in the south side of the house where Lorna's servants' room was, it was way over on the west – the oldest part of the house, next to the estate offices where members of the public never visited. Everything was dead quiet and dark outside now, so the tall windows were just shiny black surfaces. Only if you pressed your face close up against the cold glass could you see the difference between the smudgy blackness of the landscape and the cloud of the sky.

Again, there were what seemed endless corridors.

No ormolu-framed mirrors this time, the walls were Chinese wood-blocked printed papers and hung with dark-framed architectural engravings of houses with formal gardens, geometric paths, spiky conical trees and statues. They looked like pages taken from a copy of *Vitruvius Britannicus*, except these were probably originals. There were other pictures, queer mythological scenes, including one Lorna noticed of a young woman being assailed by gryphons.

Some corridors weren't lit, others glimmered with a pale green light. The floors were no longer marble or expensive wood block, they were carpet, so the silence and the whispering of the group made the progress through the building an eerie experience. The corridor turned a right angle and there was a large dark wooden door with a sloping casing above it – like the end gable of a house – and Lorna could just make out a symbol carved into the wood. It was a horizontal line intersected by two curved lines.

'I can't believe that this is going to be open.' Boone sounded sceptical.

'Well, it was earlier, I only peeped in. It's sooo creepy; I mean, look at the handle!'

Boone reached out and gripped the knob, which had been fashioned into a pineapple shape. Lorna also noticed that below the handle was a large keyhole. Boone turned the pineapple, and yes!

'Is there a light switch?' Juliet had both her hands against Boone's shoulders and was practically pushing him over the threshold.

'It's one of those old-fashioned dolly things.'

The room was illuminated with a very low light which seemed to pulse. They stepped inside and stood so close they were almost touching one another. It was unexpectedly warm, and there was an odd sweet smell – *A little like cannabis*, thought Lorna.

Lorna closed the door behind them softly while Boone and Juliet began walking round like animals pacing their cages. Kerri, Nisi and Trish were standing dead centre – at least, Lorna guessed it was "dead" because beneath their feet was a depiction of the sun god, head spiked with its fiery rays, riding a chariot drawn by four prancing horses. Freemasons; Odd Fellows; the Antediluvian Order of Buffaloes; Templars of Honour and Temperance; Rosicrucians; the Hermetic Order of the Golden Dawn. The names paraded themselves through Lorna's mind, but she had the feeling that she was on a territorial border looking into that which is so unfamiliar it is unfathomable.

After Kerri's enthusiastic description, the room seemed small to Lorna – smaller than the round church she'd once visited in Cambridge. There was a domed ceiling with golden symbols painted onto a dark ground. There were murals of the signs of the zodiac with their flowing forms and colours, looking rich and burnished in the dim wall lights which flickered, giving everything an unearthly feeling.

'I think that we should honour it with a séance.' Juliet spoke as if it was a must, offering them no alternative.

'There's no table. We need a table.' Lorna felt herself putting up an immediate resistance to the suggestion.

'We sit on the floor, like the witches of Eastwick. Think sisterhood, kiddo!'

Boone broke out in a laugh which resounded round the walls. Lorna noticed there were windows above the murals through which she thought she could see pale cloud against the dark vastness beyond. The room would be almost invisible from outside, hidden from all except those who knew.

'But that was made in Hollywood, this the back o' beyond. It'll be bloody freezing.'

Kerri bent down, put her hand to the marble, and smiled. 'No, it's not, it feels like it's got underfloor heating. Now, why would they have underfloor heating in a place like this?'

Juliet sat down right across one of the prancing horses, her long legs covered with her navy dress reaching almost to the sun's rays.

'We need some food to attract the spirits.'

'I've got one of those bread rolls.'

'Oh *look*, Boone's got his doggy bag!'

'We haven't got a candle.'

'The flickering wall lights will do. The important thing is that they're dimmed.'

'You seem to know a lot about it, Juliet.' Nisi didn't look convinced.

'The main thing is, are we all okay with it? I mean, we don't have to be full-on believers, the crucial thing is that we don't *not* believe. That weakens the spirit energy.'

'Of course we believe! We're all writers, aren't we? That means there's no limit to our imaginations.'

'It means we're convincing liars.'

'Ouch!'

'Oh, I forgot, Kerri's a *mindfulness*.'

'For now, I am. But it's okay, I believe, and I'm serious. I think we should go for it.'

'What about you, Trish?'

'I'm okay with it.'

'You look very serious.'

'That's because we need a tool. We haven't got a Ouija board or planchette.'

'Gosh, *you* seem to be well up on it.'

'Not really.'

'What about you, Boone?'

'I'm fine. If we do yes and no answers, we could ask "it" to knock, and if "it" has got a message for us, I'll write down the number of knocks and we can work out the letters later.'

'Boone's saying that 'cos he's a whizz with numbers.'

'Knock on what?'

'Well, the only hollow thing in the room is the wood panelling under the zodiac mosaics.'

'Good!' Juliet looked happy.

'Anybody got a pen and paper?' Kerri was searching in her bag.

'Pen, but no paper.'

'What do you think the bread roll is wrapped up in?'

'We're good to go; who's going to call? Juliet?'

They were making it sound more like a card game than a séance. But then, as Lorna had never taken part in a séance, she couldn't really make judgements.

'Will do. Take your time, everybody; hold the silence for a few minutes until we feel ready. Take my hands—'

'There's one problem,' interrupted Trish.

'What's that?'

'When Boone writes the numbers down, he's going to break the circle and we'll lose the spirit.'

Juliet shook her head. 'Not with this guy. What are we, bridge champion, what they call a queen or something? Hyper pattern recognition? This guy won't need to write anything down.'

'Well, I wouldn't exactly say that; I'm several thousand off the *Guinness Book of Records*,' suggested Boone modestly, 'but I'm probably good for a couple of hundred digits.'

'That's enough for us.'

They sat down forming a circle, legs outstretched, six pairs of feet almost touching, so that the rays of the mosaic sun were just visible in the space remaining in the centre, the paper serviette and bread roll placed in the middle of the sun's face. They joined hands, which steadied the group and meant that if anyone got tired, they could lean back, then pull themselves upright again by putting more pressure on their partners' hands. Lorna was holding Juliet's left hand, Trish's right hand. Next to Trish was Boone, then Nisi, with Kerri closing the circle by holding Juliet's right hand. The group fell into a deep silence, the extent of which was impossible to calculate.

Lorna's earlier misgivings were gone; once again the feeling of well-being returned which she had experienced after the course session, and she had forgiven Juliet's indiscretion earlier in the evening. Though she had never taken part in a séance, it was clear several of her companions had. It was fun, even if she was beginning to feel a little cold.

'Is there anybody there?' Juliet's voice, slow and an octave lower than usual, made Lorna almost jump out of her skin. For a moment, she had forgotten the purpose of their gathering.

Nothing.

More time passed.

'Spirit, if you're there, please make yourself known by knocking.'

Further time, impossible to measure. Lorna was feeling uncomfortably cold and it wasn't coming up from the floor – that was still warm – it was the air, it felt icy. She looked at Juliet, but her eyes were closed. *Is that what you're meant to do?* She looked at the others, who all appeared to be looking through their feet at the mosaic sun.

A further period of quiet.

There was an isolated thump and this time Lorna actually did twitch both her hands.

'You're sooo cold,' Juliet was whispering, her eyes still shut.

But the knock wasn't on the wainscotting, it was on the door, right behind Lorna. Was that it? Someone was outside wanting to come in; they would have to break the circle to answer it.

'Spirit, is that you? Are you there? If so, knock once.'

Again, a single report on the wood of the door. Lorna was shivering; she was trying hard not to, but she couldn't help it.

'Spirit, have you a message for someone here? If so, please knock to indicate letters of the alphabet.'

Lorna could feel her heart quicken; it seemed to be beating loudly, but it *wasn't* her heart making the sound, it was the door. *Knock-knock-knock*, in quick succession, then a pause of length unidentifiable, then again, *knock-knock-knock*. Lorna looked at Boone; his head was raised this time and nose pointing towards the source of the sound like a hunting dog. His eyes were closed but he seemed to have entered some kind of trance-like state. As if he was performing a dramatic impression of Mr Memory in *The Thirty-Nine Steps*. It was both comical and alarming.

A second sound was coming from somewhere very close to Lorna's head. It was the sound a patient makes when the doctor instructs you to say "Ahh". But it was horrid. Lorna looked. It was Trish. The noise was coming out of her open mouth, which was so wide open that, surely, she would damage herself? Lorna was still holding Trish's hand, but her own hand was so cold she could no longer feel Trish's. They must stop, they had to.

'Hold on, Lorna, don't let go of Trish,' hissed Juliet. 'Don't break the circle, whatever you do!'

The knocking continued, Boone still in a kind of dwam. The knocking ceased.

'Spirit, who are you?'

The knocking began again, but this time it was an uneven rhythm, like morse code. It sounded like there were two messages coming through at once. Lorna looked at Boone. His head had begun to nod as if he was struggling to separate the two messages. Further babbling was coming from Trish. But instead of it sounding as if it were coming via the epiglottis, it had a disturbing, plaintive ring to it as if it were using the roof of the mouth as a trumpet. Both lots of knocking ceased. The awful noises from Trish subsided.

'Spirit, please go in peace.'

There was a pause.

'Spirit, please go in peace.'

She'd spoken twice, but it wasn't Juliet, it was Trish who'd spoken. Lorna felt Trish's hand slip from hers.

'I'm really sorry, Juliet.'

'It's okay, but are *you* alright?' Juliet looked more overawed than offended.

'I'm fine now. It's all over.'

'How about you, Lorna? You went really cold.'

'I'm warming up. I was only in awe of the whole thing. I didn't think it would be so dramatic.'

'I don't think any of us did.' Kerri let go of Juliet and Nisi while Boone had hunched forwards, pulled the serviette from under the bread roll, snatched up the pen and was frantically writing numerals in black ink on the soft white paper.

'That's it.' Boone handed the serviette to Trish. It was covered with digits. 'It looks a mess, but it's all there. I'd work out the letters for you, but I think we should go. Also, I guess the message is for your eyes only. I hope you're okay.'

As Trish took the serviette and put it in her bag, there was a new noise. It was the unmistakable sound of a heavy key being turned in a large keyhole. Without any warning, the lights extinguished. Lorna was the nearest to the door, but she somehow knew that when she reached out, fumbled and eventually grasped hold of the brass pineapple, the door would not open.

'Here, let me try.' She felt Boone standing next to her, heard the rattling, but it was no good. 'Should we shout?'

No one spoke. It was as if they were in the grip of a strange collective pride. Nobody was prepared to shout for help.

'That wasn't an accident.' Juliet's voice had lost its enthusiastic ring. 'Whoever did that knew we were in here. They're trying to teach us a lesson.'

'There must be another way out.' Kerri sounded determined.

Lorna's heart sank. The prospect of the six of them bedding down in there was so unattractive that her mind returned to the way she had felt the moment she stepped out of the taxi, unbelievably a mere five hours ago.

6

It was possible to see shapes and form, but no detail.

'Somewhere between these two points there has to be a door, a jib door for servants, leading to the back of house.' Boone had taken charge. Lorna was conscious of his tall frame close to the wall. 'Over there is an outside wall; there won't be anything in there.' He was pointing, she was sure, but she could neither see his hand nor what he might be pointing at. Boone had obviously worked it out. 'Kerri, is that you? Can you please feel your way along the wall towards my voice. Put your hands against the wall at about shoulder height. Can you feel the wooden dado rail which runs under where the mosaic zodiac signs are?'

'Got it! What do I do now?'

'Run your hand along the underside of it and feel for a small gap between the panelling and the rail. Now, slowly come towards me and I'll do the same.'

'Nothing there.'

'Take your time; if it's not on this side of the room, it has to be on the other.'

'Sorry, no luck.' There were sounds of two bodies close together.

'Lorna, stay where you are and do the same as Kerri, walking towards me.'

Lorna could hear Boone's footsteps on the marble floor, hear his breathing, feel his warmth They stopped as he took up his next position. With her right hand above her head, Lorna was feeling her way, working from right to left searching.

'It has to be here!' As Boone spoke, Lorna could feel it. A tiny groove, less than three millimetres.

'I think it's *here*!'

'Stay there!'

Lorna could hear Boone's footsteps again, see a dark shape, feel him close to her.

'Run your hand along the groove to your left. It should turn a corner and then travel down.'

'Got it!'

'Run your hand down the groove. At some point it should be undercut and you'll feel a metal bit.'

'Got it.'

'Squeeze it towards you, then push.'

It was a door; it opened outwards. No gothic creakings; in fact, well-oiled judging by the lack of sound.

'Who's got their smartphone? Now we really need to see where we're going.'

Everyone had taken their phones to the office, as they'd been so bossily instructed to do, except, in the excitement after the course sessions, nobody had remembered to pick them up. There was a click, and Boone's hand and a small surrounding area glowed in the flame of a gas cigarette lighter.

'Thanks be to God for smokers!' It was the first time Juliet had spoken since she had lost control of the séance.

The doorway seemed to be a foot and a half wide, and only Juliet and Boone had to duck to get into what seemed to be a passageway which was tall enough for all to stand upright, but you could touch both walls either side of you without straightening your arms.

'There were no obese servants…' Boone broke off, as if he'd realised he might be sounding a bit un-PC. 'I can say that in present company.'

'Cooks were fat; it was tradition.'

'Until they caught the white plague, that is, and wasted away with consumption.'

'I'm only going to use the lighter in short bursts, so best if everyone holds on to the person in front. Pretend we're doing the conga!'

Boone was leading, followed by Trish. Nisi in front of Juliet, and Kerri with her hands round Juliet's waist. As the person who'd discovered the door, Lorna had the job of shutting it behind them. Like a human eel, they shuffled rather than slithered, slowly but steadily; the only noise being their breathing, the occasional snap of Boone's cigarette lighter, and the scraping, clonking, or rustling of their footwear crossing whatever substance the floor beneath them was made of. At first, the air smelt of that resiny scent there'd been in the zodiac room. Then it was furniture polish and, at one point, the distinct reek of overhung game. But mostly it was the untouchable but perceptible resonance of a world of antique stone, fabrics, and parchments.

Boone had solemnly instructed that they only talk in whispers. It wasn't possible to tell exactly which part of the building they were passing through. At any time, they could be only inches away from other humans who might be innocently sleeping, reading, chatting. Or perhaps the escapers could be close to the nerve centre of the house where those in charge were planning the next day's events, charging up smartphones, or – more worryingly – ensuring guests kept the curfew, whatever that might involve. *What is going on here?* Lorna asked herself. The contrast between the professional real-world delivery of the course tutors and the forced drama of the people who were supposed to be running the house was, so far, unexplainable.

She was glad she'd spoken up for that girl, but what was going to happen next? Anybody could see that "Spraycat" was absolutely furious. She'd stood up to him; he'd had to give way and agree to speak to that girl in private. He'd known damn well it hadn't been Lorna who'd made the comment about porn actors, but she'd drawn attention to herself by siding with the tubby girl. Lorna would not be forgiven for that. There *was* something going on here: the two-way mirrors, somebody – probably Spraycat – locking them in the zodiac room. There had to be more to it than mildly abusive theatrical antics designed to excite and entertain.

Lorna had allowed her mind to drift and found herself almost falling on top of Juliet. The human eel was attempting to descend a spiral staircase. The stair was wider than most of the corridors they had so far negotiated, and she had strayed too close into the wynde of the stair.

'Hold on, kiddo!'

Lorna's mood was shifting like a roller coaster. She'd been elated to discover the door, to escape the prospect of the six of them spending the night without access to toilets. But, after traversing another wider corridor with a rough wood-boarded floor and plaster walls, they began to stagger down a second stair and Lorna could feel herself edging towards panic. They must be going further away from the dining and breakout rooms. She had a strong sensation that the group had fallen into a world away from that which they'd escaped, and that they seemed unable to break through the membrane which separated those two worlds. Surely there'd been other jib doors on their route, alternative ways back to the front of house; they couldn't go on like this forever? The little procession came to a rapid halt, there were several bursts from Boone's lighter, muted thumpings, and then the dull glow of electric light fell across their faces. Boone ducked and stepped ringingly onto a fine marble floor.

'Apologies for taking you round the houses! I didn't want to risk bumping into the goons. I'm pretty sure that this is the hallway in which the commercial visitors arrive, so it's deserted.'

They had emerged from a door similar to that through which they'd entered the servant's network, but this time it was under a grand stair. There were marble busts on plinths standing on the floor, tight up against the wall. To get past the staircase, they had to keep in single file as they passed the sculptures. Nobody was speaking; it seemed that all had had sufficient adventure for one day. Lorna followed the group up the grand stair, across a hollow-sounding wood block floor, through a chamber of tall glass-fronted cabinets containing antique pots, and along a narrow gallery lined with more busts on plinths. In the dimmed electric light, it looked eerie.

'We all know our way from here!'

They were once again standing in the Great Hall, with its giant and mysterious painted surfaces.

'Goodnight, all!' Boone raised his hand and walked up one of the twin staircases. The others followed. At the top, he paused, turned, and added, 'Oh, oh… I'm afraid we left the bread roll!'

Lorna found herself walking the wooden flight of stairs to the second floor with Trish, who also had an individual room there. As they said goodnight, Trish put her hand in her bag and pulled out the paper serviette.

'I'm not really a medium, but I went on a mediumship course, and I didn't realise I had any ability until this evening.' She handed the serviette to Lorna. 'The message wasn't for me. It was for you.'

'Thank you.' Lorna automatically took the paper. As she did so, she could feel the warmth draining from her face.

'I need to tell you that there were two spirits who visited us this evening. The first was a good spirit; it was for you, personal, and of course I can't be sure, but I believe that the message will be in the positive interests of your welfare. That spirit departed in peace and went to the Light, but the second spirit was a rogue and it did not go. It's still here, Lorna. Again, I can't be sure, but sometimes they latch onto a good spirit in order to enter our world. I think it was what is sometimes called a "home spirit", in that it's to do with this house rather than you. I seriously don't believe that it can harm you, but please, *do* take extra care.'

Lorna didn't know what to say. It was staggering.

'Are you alright?' That was the second time in six hours someone had asked Lorna that question.

'I could stay with you a while, if you like?' It *was* a question.

'I'm going to be fine. A good night's sleep for both of us!' Lorna managed a smile.

'I'm just along the corridor if you're not.'

'Thanks, I appreciate it.'

'Goodnight!'

'Goodnight!'

This time it wasn't panic which Lorna experienced; it was fear, a deep and distant memory which, for the first time in the last six hours, she had to admit to herself that there might, might, might be some justification for.

7

It was 07.30. Lorna was standing, staring at the outside of the little secret door which all six of them had trouped through in their escape only eight hours ago. She'd decided to have a wander before breakfast, awoken early partly because she was raring to go for the course, but also because, quite frankly, given the happenings of last night, a longer period of sleep was impossible.

Just who is Golightly? And what about his nasty sidekick, Spraycat? When she returned home, she would research them. What mattered now was the course. She'd also decided to put on one side thoughts about what had happened in the zodiac room. She would decode the message – if there really was a message – when she had more time, and that very likely wouldn't be before she left Golightly.

She squeezed past a larger-than-life stone bust of Dionysus, its hair depicted like wriggling worms and its huge nose *quite repulsive!* Up the staircase into the chamber with the Etruscan – or whatever they were – pots. The whole place felt like a tomb. Across the wood floor, onto the black and white marble floor, and at the end of the next chamber there was a window with sunlight. Sunlight, that's what Lorna wanted. She couldn't go outside – not yet. So, she would go and stand in that lovely patch of sun. She'd dressed up a bit today. Put on a skirt, an all-in-one shifty thing with a turn-over collar. It was dark plaid and, with a navy cardigan over it and black stockings, she thought it looked quite "Bloomsbury". Away had gone the loafers and out had come some black heels – not stilettos, but quite dressy in an off-beat way. Good grief! She wouldn't have dressed like this when she was at Jay Natal's, it was always slick suits there – for her, French or Italian.

It was the gallery they'd walked down last night, the one with windows along one side and marble busts lining the other, but what a contrast! Instead of the rectangles of black shiny glass, there were bars of light running across the floor. The whole corridor looked golden. The only movement was tiny dust motes she could see drifting from one side of the space to the other.

A figure appeared round the corner at the end of the gallery. As it stepped into one of the bars of light, she could see it was Spreighmont. He was strolling, while she was standing and feeling embarrassed because he'd caught her unawares. He was patrolling – doing his job, no doubt, but that didn't stop her feeling like an intruder into his world, overawed by the antiquities which surrounded her.

Everything about the man signalled that he was thinking that all he could see around him was for his benefit. His double-breasted suit, slim tie, and white button-down shirt should be grateful for having such a personage as *he* moving and breathing within them. Even his black Oxfords, which, by the sound of it, he'd had steel-tipped, seemed to be tap-dancing to his tune. As he came nearer, passing through each untouchable shaft of light, there was a slight stroboscopic effect, and Lorna had the distinct impression that the marble head of each Roman emperor nodded in appreciation of his presence. She carried on walking, wondering if she should say anything other than the courtesy of a greeting. Something she couldn't quite express flashed through her mind. Was she swaying her hips a little bit too much as she walked? As the two of them drew level, she opened her mouth to speak, but the man had already spoken. It was so quick. She hadn't taken in what he'd actually said until the two had passed one another.

'Not with you!' She managed to get her reply out.

She kept walking, didn't look back. Her response sounded miserably defensive. He'd just made a lewd suggestion, for God's sake; it was an assault. She should be giving him hell; just what did she think she was doing? Still, she kept walking, didn't turn to look at him. There was silence behind her. He'd stopped, was watching her. She reached the end of the gallery and, again without looking, turned the corner, slipped between the plinths of two stone busts and leant against the wall. She could feel the coolness of the stone against the back of her head, heard the *tap*, *tap* of the steel-tipped Oxfords going away from her. She shut her eyes.

She would complain, of course. But to whom? Golightly? They were cronies. To the tutors? That was a different world, the real world. This was a kingdom of make-believe; the product it was delivering was professional enough, but the essence of its organisation was bogusness, it was show business. She was trapped. The police? That would only create trouble for herself. She could leave, of course; walk out. Not bloody likely! She was here to develop her creativity. She'd paid a stratospheric sum of money and now she was being subjected to abuse by the organisers. She was the client, for God's sake; they were the suppliers! But the way it seemed was that they were masters and she was their servant.

That's how these people worked. That was the modus operandi of the predator: make themselves untouchable by creating a situation which is so unreal that anyone who questions it seems fake and implausible themselves. And the way he'd said it, just as if he was offering some dainty, "Fancy a quick mince pie?".

Suddenly, she didn't feel safe at all. Her first thought was to go back to her room. But there was no lock on the door. People! She would go where people were. At least he wouldn't try anything if others were around. She found herself making for the dining room, but it was twenty minutes before breakfast and the room was deserted save for a solitary Betty putting finishing touches to the buffet. She passed through to the breakout room. There was one person there: Juliet. There was no hiding. Lorna's face said something was amiss even if it didn't tell the whole story.

'Hello, are you *alright*?'

That question, again. For a fleeting moment she thought she would tell Juliet everything, but she stopped herself.

'It's those bush fires, I'm worried about Matt – and his house.'

It wasn't only Juliet's indiscretion at yesterday's supper, nor her losing control of the séance. In the short period she'd known her, Lorna had discovered things about Juliet which were making her wary. She'd found that she was in favour of the reintroduction of the death penalty, she was of the opinion that husbands should dominate their wives, that there were too many women in the UK workplace and, worst of all, that in ninety-nine per cent of rape cases the woman was to blame. But in that very instant, Lorna made an important decision. When all the others were sitting and chatting about the events of the day in the breakout room that evening after 10.00, she would leave the house, walk up to Cracklewood, the reservoir, and phone Chas. She wouldn't go into details, that would be a trap too easy to fall into, and it would sound like hysteria. She would merely ask him to find out something about Golightly and Spreighmont. Chas would welcome doing a bit of digging – there could even be a story in it for him.

8

'We can't be the only bunch of students who find the management here creepy.' It was the voice of Juliet. She and Lorna were relaxing on the generous leather Chesterfields after a rewarding day of course classes, buffet lunch, coffee and tea breaks, a successful and much appreciated supper, prepared, cooked and served by the first group, and followed by a hilarious presentation by their course tutor, Ed, talking about his struggle to get published. Sitting close by were other students with whom Lorna had managed to start various conversations as the day progressed. There were Drew, Jenna and Nina from creative writing. Also from creative writing was

Debbie "from Devon", according to Elton John the busybody taxi driver, one piece of information which had actually proved authentic. From transcendental meditation there was Diane Viggiano, who was sitting near Lorna but on a different sofa. The others were all piled on the one giant sofa, the four girls sitting in a row on the seats, and Boone and Drew perched on each of its wide arms. Lorna couldn't help noticing that Diane had her hair in exactly the same bobbed style which Lorna had before the end of the first virus lockdown, when she'd had it pixied. There was also something else about Diane which Lorna couldn't quite put her finger on. They hadn't talked, but they would – Lorna would make sure of that.

Of course, she hadn't said a damn thing to anyone about that bastard Spraycat. Though he'd already come up in the conversations frequently. Mr Snappy, Groucho, Creep Features were some of the tags already hung on him. Drew had an interesting take.

'Deuterostome. All humans are deuterostomes insofar as when they develop in the womb, the anus forms before any other opening. Which means at one point we were nothing but arseholes. Some people never develop beyond that point.'

Much hilarity. Lorna laughed, but imagine what the reaction would be if she told *her* story about what had happened at 7.40 this morning. Some disbelief, probably minimal empathy, more likely the unspoken consensus would be: here's a person who just wants to draw attention to themselves. Sir John Spreighmont, a clever fucker indeed! No, Lorna would not look for an ally, she would proceed with her plan. Chas was hardly an investigative journalist. If he were analysing reasons why Golightly achieved world status as a nature reserve, or ferreting out information on why its two lakes attracted more than twenty-five species of bird, or finding out the name of the local woodsman who made the country's first sighting of the amicable warbler, Chas would be your man. But dodgy dealings at the heart of what was quite possibly once the seat of the flower of the English aristocracy? Lorna wasn't so sure, but she needed help and Chas was always good at providing that. He wasn't always her pillar of strength, but he wasn't far from being that.

Which was the reason why she was sitting – and perhaps a little apprehensively – on the leather Chesterfield, dressed in black chinos and navy-blue cashmere. Not quite commando gear, but it would lessen the risk of her being spotted by hawk-like eyes, Mr Snappy-type eyes. She'd changed at lightning speed after supper before the evening course session, and she fancied she could see Juliet eyeing her strangely. *Well, think on, kiddo!*

'Rumour has it that Golightly is ex-MI5.'

It seemed that everybody had heard that one, so Boone wasn't telling anybody anything they hadn't known – or at least considered. He was probably only saying it to test everybody out, get them thinking.

'After that impromptu tour of the house you gave us yesterday evening, anybody might say that you know your way round here *rather* too well, Boone. How can we be sure you're not a *mole*?'

'Ouch, Juliet!'

Debbie and those not in the know about the previous evening's events were puzzled.

'It's a joke,' corrected Lorna before anybody else got the chance to tell the tale and add too much detail. 'A few of us did some exploring yesterday and got ourselves lost. Boone here used his amazing powers of spatial geometry to get us back to base.'

'It was nothing! But you're right, I could easily be a mole, keeping tabs on you all, watching how you react to their little tricks, reporting back. Any of us could be.'

'Is he really a lord and does he own the house? The way he was going on, you'd think it'd been in the family for generations.' Jenna was curious.

'The title is the land and the land is the title,' said Juliet.

'It mentions a charitable trust in the course literature,' said Boone. 'There're a number of names of trustees but his isn't one of them. Most likely, "Golightly" is a pseudonym; he's probably just the house manager playacting.'

'Trust is the least appropriate word; I wouldn't trust any of them,' said Nina.

'As far as I can gather,' expanded Boone, 'the trust is set up to manage the estate. There's another foundation who we paid our fee to. That seems to fund itself through grants and donations. There's a list of benefactors – they're actors, rock stars, and so forth.'

'That's the bit I *do* trust,' said Nina. 'Those are real names, real people, it's the real world, and they don't just donate to Golightly. There's also the house; it has a history, it's packed with collected antiquities which are catalogued. No doubt they appear in learned journals and are referred to at length in literature. That's all real as well. There're the other businesses on the estate: the garden centre, the arboretum, the private parties, the musical events and the weddings. They're all genuine. But if you look at the guidebook, the house was built by the Earl of Parksfield; there's the Galburgh family mentioned and a Charles Golightly. I'm not a genealogist or historian, and you'd have to look closely into it, but there's only one mention of Golightly, so land and title are not exactly interchangeable, Juliet. I have a feeling that our pussycat lord is a fake. It's as if "Golightly" is a new invention – a kind of rebranding. What do you think, Lorna? You mentioned you were in marketing.'

Lorna had been so busy thinking about her task ahead that she suddenly didn't know what to say. She had not read the guidebook to Golightly – she hadn't even properly read the course literature. She began to blether.

'Everybody can reinvent themselves at any time. Everything can be reinvented.' She was also fighting to regain her equilibrium after hearing Nina mention Parksfield. That was it, that's what it had been called!

It was another surge of memory. Then it was gone. 'History is always written by the status quo. I'm rambling, I know, and I'm no historian, but I was reading a phrase in a newspaper article the other day: "The reason why almost no one has ever heard of the Battle of Towton, when the Yorkists practically wiped out the Lancastrians in the English Wars of the Roses, is that by the time that piece of history came to be written, it was written by – or for – the royal Tudor dynasty who didn't like the Yorkists." The only battle that anybody knows anything about was the Battle of Bosworth, where Richard of York was killed and the Tudors took power.'

Lorna was suddenly aware that all six faces were turned and studying her as if she were some sort of sage, including Diane on the next Chesterfield, who hadn't said a word. Everybody, it seemed, had heard of the Battle of Bosworth – at least, the battle where Richard III was killed – but nobody had heard of the Battle of Towton or even knew where it was.

'So, you rewrite history in order to maintain the status quo or create a new one?' Drew sounded as if he was choosing his words with care.

'Or to discredit the dodgy.'

'So, has Golightly – or Parksfield – got a dodgy past? Rebellion? Slavery connections?'

'I don't know, but there's another possibility. Piggybacking.' Lorna's head was clearing a bit, but she was determined to shine. Again, all eyes seemed to be on her. 'Like in the rebranding of products – say, perfume or cars, or anything. You create a new product; it has no provenance, so no kudos. So, you find an established revered brand. No need to buy them like BMW did with Morris Motors, just "collaborate" with them like Swatch did with Mercedes to produce the Smart Car. That kind of thing is acceptable and above board, but there's examples of those – I can't mention – who infiltrate.'

'So, what you're suggesting, in either case,' said Boone in a conspiratorial kind of voice, 'is that a house with a history – which may or may not have a suspect past – has been infiltrated by persons or elements which are seeking a new status – i.e. Golightly and his dubious henchman – and that's all hunky-dory with the various trusts and foundations because it's making a new reputation for them?'

'And a load of money!'

'Something like that.'

'Taking a slightly different tack, there's another possibility,' suggested Jenna. 'Remember that guy, Radovan Karadzic, a psychiatrist who served as President of Republika Srpska and was wanted for war crimes? After the Bosnian War, he vanished; they couldn't find him for years until one day someone spotted him working in a Belgrade psychiatric clinic as a specialist in alternative therapy for sexual disorders.'

'You think Golightly could be a wanted man?' Drew sounded excited.

'I'm just taking up Lorna's point about self-reinvention – that and the power of hiding in plain sight.'

'Or it could all be pure theatre,' insisted Drew. 'We pay a fabulous sum of money to stay at a Baroque palace in the middle of nowhere for five days while we get all creative, mindful, assertive, and transcendental. They provide an additional atmosphere of drama. They're only actors – probably nice people really!'

Lorna almost said something, but stopped herself and gave way to Nina.

'It's true, it's all acting; the sensory deprivation trick on the first evening and the regimentation of the helpers. Has anybody else noticed how they're *all* called Betty? They probably each have numbers like those legions of hotel workers in Eastern Bloc countries before the fall of the Berlin Wall. As a visitor, you'd walk up and down the hotel stairs and there'd be dozens of them all polishing the stair balustrades or, outside, scores of them in lines sweeping snow – even though it was going to snow again that evening. A conspicuous show of full employment, nobody actually seeming to be in charge, but ruled rigidly – all the power from the top, in the hands of a relative few.'

'An MI5 background may have a cosy armchair frisson for some,' Jenna insisted, 'but don't forget that in any intelligence system, situations arise where people have to be disposed of for the survival of the many; one person makes a decision to have another killed – sometimes a person who is on their side. I'm not saying it shouldn't happen, spying is necessary, but it's not a virtue.'

'Of course, everybody knows it was the Americans who won World War II.' Boone stretched himself as he sat on the arm of the Chesterfield as if he was astride a horse, one booted foot resting on the stone floor at the side of the sofa, the other stockinged foot drawn up, toes digging into the front of the deep-buttoned arm. The other boot was standing upright on a Bokhara rug, which was in front of the sofa. It seemed apparent to Lorna that Boone's tongue was provocatively in his cheek. 'But so did spying help win the war. You Brits! Of all the German spies operating in Britain in the lead up to D-Day, guess how many were double agents? Some? No, *all* of them. Britain had the monopoly on spies. You could say it's the British speciality.'

'It's the deceit of it that gets me,' said Debbie. 'I don't want to sound like a piss-pot of sanctimoniousness – to quote Elizabeth I – but what's the point of living a life pretending you're something you're not?'

'Who doesn't do that?' Juliet scoffed.

'Or pretending not to be something you *are?*'

'It must take a very specific type of personality.'

'Someone who enjoys taking risks, of which the consequences could well lead to a violent end to your life.'

'A sociopath – in some cases even a psychopath?'

'I think you've got to be careful not to over type-cast people.' Drew was sitting on the other arm of the sofa and leaning his head against the backrest. He was practically lying down, both feet sticking out over the end of the arm. He was looking intensely serious. '"Every concentration camp guard was a psychopath." That's what we believed – until the film *The Reader* came along. A few of them probably were, but the majority were – like the character in the film – not very intelligent people, often illiterate, applying for a job – of which they usually didn't know the details – in order to better themselves in life. After all, those jobs weren't being advertised by some underground gangster organisation. They were being offered by government, so, to all intents and purposes, they were above board! It's always the regime you have to be wary of, rather than the individual.'

'There have been spies forever, it's a way of life,' said Nina. 'It's the method that I don't like. I mean, do we really have to have all this surveillance?'

'I know these courses are exclusive in that you pay a lot of money for them, but the management know a lot about us all. It almost feels like we're being hand-picked for something,' said Juliet.

'And what about the questionnaire we all had to fill in,' said Jenna. 'It was like applying for a Russian visa!'

'They need our dietary requirements, medication and medical history, bank account details, vaccination status.' Juliet was looking and sounding as if she'd organised the questionnaire herself.

'That's the age of information,' insisted Boone. 'It's just something we have to accept. Look at all the personal stuff they – I mean organisations in general – have got on us. It means they can build models, make predictions, analyse people's buying habits. All the bumf and gumph they've now got on people regarding virus pandemics. It means they can be better prepared when a worse pandemic comes along, which we now know it will.'

'But it's too much, I sometimes feel that my smartphone is spying on me. It knows where I've been, which shops, parks, even which bus stops I've walked past.'

'You can switch that app off, Nina.'

'But why should I? And I'm not alone in that opinion. How many people in the world have got mobile phones? Answer – according to Statista – seventy-five per cent. But that can't be right. What they mean is that out of the world population of 7.8 billion, there are 5.8 billion mobile phones in circulation – a lot of people have several. That's a hell of a lot of surveillance… and influence. The likes of Google rule the world. I want information without being spied on.'[i]

'I'm afraid that's a contradiction in terms,' said Drew with authority. 'Also, just because you've got that command switched off doesn't mean to say information's not being collected and you're not under surveillance.'

'There's far too much porn on the internet.' Juliet was sounding just a little righteous.

'It's too easily available,' Drew in agreement, 'except, rather like alcohol and drugs, I'm *afraid*, it's not going to get less available, only more. That's it with practically everything, so prepare yourself. It's like rising numbers of cars on roads, you're stuck with it. You can't ban it. The only way forward is to educate people to cope. One solution…' – and here Drew's tongue sounded as if it had strayed into his cheek – 'instead of trying to limit supply of porn, why not legislate to refine consumption? The real problem is there're too many wrong-minded people watching porn. For instance, in the UK, you used to need a licence to own a dog; why not a compulsory licence to watch porn? Not a paying kind of licence, say, you simply have to pass a test, not just a box-ticking exercise, a genuine exam like an application to a private club with a proposer and seconder.'

Some laughter here.

'You do it from the top, through government, you put the pressure on the service provider – not the suppliers of the porn. The service providers are the most powerful people in the supply chain, already they bully the consumer into upgrading their smartphone accounts by making their phones crash.'

'I wondered why my phone is always crashing.'

'The government could make it worth the service provider's while using taxpayer's money to enforce.'

Hoots of laughter.

'That's dictatorship by social engineering.'

'So? We've got that already in the form of multiple surveillance through our smartphones,' Drew continued. 'The licence test would be all geared around ability with social skills. So those who were good social mixers, got themselves out frequently to meet new people, would pass with flying colours, whereas miserable couch potatoes watching more than twenty-five hours of TV a week, addicted to computer and smartphone games, and even those with a snobby penchant for online bridge tournaments—'

'Hold on! Are you trying to get at me or something, Drew?'

'With faceless opponents on the other side of the world, just wouldn't qualify for the ticket. I mean, giving a licence to watch porn to that sort of mindset is like giving a bottle of gin to a three-year-old.'

'Don't you get bitchy with me, Drew!'

The two male Americans were dialoguing from one arm of the sofa to the other, the faces of the four girls between them like spectators at a tennis match. Lorna couldn't decide whether this was a genuine altercation or banter. Sometimes she couldn't even follow who was saying what. It didn't matter. The whole atmosphere of the place was one of staged dramas; it was getting to them all. It almost felt as if the house was drawing thoughts out of them and that as soon as those thoughts had been spoken that they became the property of Golightly and no longer belonged to he who had spoken them. Maybe Juliet was right: they were all being lined up for something, and Boone and Drew were a couple of moles trying to draw them out. Perhaps the selection would be made at the end of the course? Awkward laughter all round, with some harrumphing from Nina.

'Food for thought, Drew, but totally unpoliceable.'

'We're already being policed, Nina! It'll happen, you'll see. Now, would you like me to tell my pizza story?' Drew was looking mischievous.

'You don't have to say yes to cookies.'

'You do if you want the information.'

'Alright, don't have a smartphone then!'

'Oh, come on, Juliet!'

'People are always complaining about their "rights of privacy" being spied on, having their personal information being misused. But if you've nothing to hide, then, surely, you've got nothing to fear?'

'Would you like me to tell my pizza story?'

'Yes!' All.

'Oh, I didn't ask you to say "yes".' Drew was looking more mischievous.

'Alright, go on!'

'Oh, I didn't ask you to say "go on".' Drew was behaving like he was playing annoyingly hard to get.

'It's never as simple as that, Juliet.'

'I asked you if you would like me to tell you my pizza story.' Drew, smug.

'Why should the idea of Big Brother always be negative? When we're small, our parents watch over us. Why shouldn't there be a body or organisation that watches over us when we're adults?' Juliet was leaning forwards and looking directly at Boone.

'MI5, MI6 and the CIA do that, so, for that matter, did England's George III's SS (Secret Service), syphon off money – taxpayer's money – to finance and ensure the effective passing of the Act of Union between Great Britain and Ireland. All these groups stop us getting invaded, help to prevent terrorists planting bombs.'

'So, the establishing of the United Kingdom was

the work of England's Secret Service?' Nina looked incredulous. 'How do you know this, Boone?'

'Because he's an historical researcher for the BBC!' It would appear that Boone and Drew had done a bit of preparation on this point.

'We've proved it through documentary evidence. Here's another example, maybe more relevant to the history of Golightly. George III – same English monarch – borrowed money from Drummond's Bank in London to finance a campaign that would ensure the success of the Pitt government, effectively to rig an election. Unbelievable? Just wait till you hear the next point. Who was Drummond? The bank still exists; it's private but part of NatWest. Drummonds were a Scots family, Jacobites. Evidence reveals that Drummond – the banker's father – tried to kill George II (George the III's grandfather) by fighting at the Battle of Culloden in 1746. As we know, the Scots lost the battle, and Father Drummond was killed; had he not been killed in battle, he would likely have been captured and could well have been hanged, drawn and quartered for treason. I think we'd all agree that borrowing money from your grandfather's would-be assassin isn't illegal, it's business, but taking it to the point of hypocrisy? We've turned up literally scores of similar examples of how the English ruling class maintained their status quo by acts which might be considered amoral or even downright corrupt. It happened and it's still going on right now. You Brits are in for a shock!'

'That's a bit patronising, Boone. I'm thinking

less political, less tangible, if you like.' It looked to Lorna that Juliet felt she was losing control again; the American contingent of Boone and Drew seemed formidable – almost threatening.

'What, God?' Boone sounded like he was sneering.

'Or like Mother Carey in *The Water Babies*?' Drew's voice seemed contemptuous.

'Not *quite* as intangible as that, more like guardian angels but in physical form and with a non-partisan brief, for a common good.'

'Ha! No such thing, Juliet. It's always based on motive; it either has to be economic or ideological, there's no halfway house.'

'Put all your trust in the state. You're taking a big risk. As Drew says, it's the regime you have to be careful of.'

'I blame the Tories!' shouted Jenna. It seemed to Lorna that she was parodying.

'I know you're being funny, Jenna,' said Boone, 'but what you've hit on there says it all. It's the classic statement that closes down all creative discussion. People can't think of anything else to say so they say, "If Labour had done this or the Tories hadn't done that." Party politics is the best – and quite possibly the only – system we've got, but it limits thinking. It's how the status quo – be it the ruling classes or whoever – manipulate people. It's what the Romans called "bread and circuses". "Give the people something to keep them entertained or take their minds off the bigger picture. Keep people on the surface, stop them digging deeper. Give them hustings!".'

'I don't disagree,' said Debbie, 'but just going back to the issue of surveillance for a moment – it's up to individual choice, you just have to be careful about what you buy.'

'Don't tell me, Debbie, that every time you buy a T-shirt, you research where it's been made, who made it, how many gallons of water, how many tons of CO_2 went into its production. You trust the manufacturer.'

'Social media's a form of surveillance.' Lorna desperately felt it was time for her to say something again. 'Networking is a force for good in business, sharing business contacts is the way to get more business. How thinking has changed! Remember the days when leaking the company client list was a sackable offence. It's the other way round now; it's the way to get *more* business. Now, you're more likely to get promotion for leaking information than get fired. People can't expect to cut themselves off and live in their own ivory towers.'

'There's massive change coming in the world in the next fifty years.' Boone was leaning forward, his hands working into the deep-buttoned leather crevices of the Chesterfield. It was as if the good-humoured conveyor of the séance message and their saviour from the zodiac room of the previous evening had been replaced with a prophet of terrible tidings, and for one moment Lorna thought this conversation was going to go on forever, and she might have to abandon her little proposed nocturnal adventure. The leather of the Chesterfield squeaked submissively as Boone hammered out his theory. 'We think that the information revolution we're in at present is momentous, but it's nothing compared to what's coming. We're running out of time. The harvesting of earth's resources to fund growth has way exceeded its capacities and we're heading for "total societal collapse". Reliable sources dating back to 1972 suggest such a disintegration happening in 2040. In practice, we can't be sure *exactly* when or what the rate of collapse will be, all we know is that it *will* happen. The next eighteen years are critical, not to avert climate change or slow down global warming – because whatever we do won't make any palpable difference – but what really counts is to clarify who is the status quo, and how will it maintain its position as life becomes increasingly tribal. I say it again, you Brits are in for a terrible shock, particularly the armchair-sitting *Guardian* readers, the uni-educated so-called elite—'

'Of which you're a member!' snapped Juliet in a flash.

'Fer-sure, fer-sure…' Boone parodying his countrywomen by lapsing into Californian Valleyspeak. 'But remember the way the Brexit vote in 2016 went? Events like that are a taste of things to come.'

Nina's eyebrows raised in what could be an "I'm taking this with a pinch of salt" attitude, but Lorna could see Juliet's mouth puckered into an angry ring. Boone forged on.

'There's a schism opening up in British society, divisions not easily recognisable, nowhere near as historically straightforward as the aristocracy ensuring that the working classes didn't have a vote in the eighteenth century. Not half as simple as the British government passing laws to prevent the Chartists from getting power in the nineteenth century. The rift we're looking at today isn't being caused by AI; it's something much more traditionally industrial than that: it's the motor car. It's between those who may only use it occasionally because they live in big cities which have alternative ways of getting around, and those who live in provincial towns and the country who are one hundred per cent dependent on car travel. It's not a north/south divide; it's London and the rest of the country—'

'No, no, no!' Juliet was shaking her dark bobbed head.

'But the coming conflict isn't between those two groups *just because* they live in different parts of the country, or because they're from varying social class backgrounds. *They're* basically the same people. The war – and don't misunderstand me, I'm not talking about the streets turning to "rivers of blood"; there's no need for that, not with the power of social media – is between those who deal the motor car, those who fix the motor car, those who fuel the motor car – i.e. the supermarkets – and those who make the laws in Britain. And where are those laws made?'

'Westminster…' Debbie looked across at Juliet and hesitated.

Juliet looked as if she was going to explode. Of course she would. During one of their little tête-à-têtes, Lorna had gathered that not only had they gone to the same school, but that Juliet's father was the proud owner of a string of Ford car dealers. She would not take kindly to the transatlantic Boone's fanciful notion that her dad and thousands like him – those who dealt, fixed and fuelled the motor car – had emerged as a new and heretofore invisible aristocracy, were exercising feudal power over rural and provincial Britain's poor defenceless car-dependent residents, and were a threat to its government.

'The laws are decided in London, from Westminster!' Jenna seemed to be on top of Boone's reasoning. 'The UK has never had proper devolution, so ultimately central government is still in control, but all those in the provinces who are connected in some shape or form with supplying, servicing and fuelling the motor car have become a very powerful group indeed and a threat to regional and ultimately central government. I can see that.'

'And most local councillors are patsies for the dealers, fixers and fuellers!' Nina was adamant.

'You're all talking utter and complete rubbish!' Juliet's feet stamped so hard on the Bokhara rug that Lorna could hear a slapping echoing sound from the stone paving on which the rug had so snugly lain. Lorna thought Juliet was going to get up and march out of the room, and for the first time it occurred to her that Juliet might have chosen the wrong course. Mindfulness for anger management issues might have been more apt. In the seismic vibration, Boone's solitary abandoned boot had fallen onto its side on the Bokhara.

'I think I need to tell my pizza story. Before we all fall out.'

'Come on, Drew, he needs to tell his pizza story.' Debbie.

'Yes, for God's sake, tell us your pizza story!' Somebody.

'Oh, I didn't ask you to blaspheme.' Drew was appearing outrageously self-righteous.

Silence.

'Oh, I didn't ask you to be silent...' Drew, insufferable.

But Boone's argument wasn't *entirely* mad as far as Lorna could see. Chas had, for some time, been saying that the motor barons had become too powerful without practically anybody noticing. They were an undue influence on an unsuspecting, creatures-of-habit, car-dependent provincial and rural British public – according to Gov UK, 9.7 million of the UK population lived in rural areas and 46.9 million lived in urban areas, but worldwide this figure was fifty-one per cent living in urban areas and forty-nine per cent living in rural areas. Undoubtedly, those who dealt, fixed and fuelled the motor car had the upper hand – world dominance perhaps? Matching Thorpe wasn't exactly deep country and was only a few miles from London's underground Central line, but Lorna had watched TV news, read things, and gathered that provincial councillors – cross party – were unanimously voting against the imposition of traffic congestion charges. She'd seen Green Party councillors losing seats right across the provinces, noticed that retail forums were campaigning to get inner city parking fees reduced. She'd seen provincial "green belts" being violated, been amazed at how many road-widening and carriageway-dualling schemes had been approved. Couldn't understand why so many pedestrianisation schemes in provincial towns were being promoted and trumpeted as exemplars of town planning, but then mysteriously abandoned. Something was going on; muscle was being used, councillor's arms were being twisted. It wasn't right.

'Please, Drew, if you don't tell us your pizza story, we're going to have a collective nervous breakdown.'

'It's a telephone conversation between a customer wanting to order a pizza and an organisation called… let's call it Ogle.'

'Go on, Drew.'

'Oh, I didn't ask you to say "go on".'

'Shh! Don't upset him.'

'CALLER: Is this Pizza Hat?

'OGLE: No, sir, it's Ogle Pizza.

'CALLER: Sorry, must have dialled the wrong number.

'OGLE: No, sir, Ogle bought Pizza Hat last week.

'CALLER: Okay, I'd like to order a pizza.

'OGLE: Do you want your usual, sir?

'CALLER: Usual? Do you know me?

'OGLE: According to our caller ID data, the last twenty times you ordered an extra-large with three cheeses, sausage, pepperoni, mushrooms and meatballs on a thick crust.

'CALLER: Great! That's what I'll have.

'OGLE: May I suggest that this time you order a pizza with ricotta, arugula, sun-dried tomatoes and olives on a whole wheat gluten-free thin crust?

'CALLER: I don't want a vegetarian pizza.

'OGLE: You have high cholesterol, sir.

'CALLER: How the hell do you know?

'OGLE: We cross-referenced your medical records with your home phone number. We have your blood test results for the last seven years.

'CALLER: Look, I don't want your vegetarian pizza, I already take medication for my cholesterol.

'OGLE: Excuse me, sir. You have not taken your medication regularly. According to our database, you purchased only one box of thirty tablets from Floyds pharmacy four months ago.

'CALLER: I bought more from another pharmacy.

'OGLE: That doesn't show on your credit card statement.

'CALLER: I paid cash.

'OGLE: According to your bank statement, you didn't draw cash.

'CALLER: I have other sources of cash.

'OGLE: That doesn't show on your latest tax returns, unless you bought them using an undeclared income source, which is against the law!

'CALLER: What the hell!

'OGLE: I'm sorry, sir, but we only use such information in order to help you.

'CALLER: Enough! I'm sick to death of search

engines, social media, apps, and the rest. I'm going to an island without TV, internet, where there's no phone, and no one to watch or spy on me.

'OGLE: I understand perfectly, sir, but you'll need to renew your passport. It expired six weeks ago.'

Appropriate hilarity, with murmurs of "Quite right!" and "Some good points", and "The price of information progress!".

'By the way, it's not really *my* story, I didn't make it up. I'm surprised nobody's heard it before; it's all over the internet, on practically every site with a joker's corner, and probably sitting in your inboxes from someone you know right now.'

'Well, I don't like the way that they look at us.' At last, Lorna had said it – nowhere near as much as she wanted to say, but sufficient to be controversial, raise future questions.

'I agree!' It was Diane. Okay, Lorna had been quiet – she was nervous thinking about what she was going to be doing over the next half hour – but Diane hadn't said a word, just sat on her own on the adjoining sofa.

'And on that note, thanks, Drew, for the story, and to all, for the stimulating discussion, even if I didn't always follow who was saying what! I'm whacked so I'm turning in. Sleep well!'

'You look as if you're going on manoeuvres.' Juliet was looking at Lorna's heavy-duty trainers. The comment was meant for Lorna alone, but with the banter among the others still going on it was doubtful that anybody else had heard. So what if Juliet was suspicious? Ask yourself why, kiddo!

As Lorna left the room, she saw Diane follow. If Lorna put a spurt on as she walked through the dining room, up the stairs to the Great Hall, she would be out of the glazed front entrance door before Diane even appeared at the top of the stairs.

9

Before Lorna had even closed the glass-panelled door behind her, she was regretting her clothing choice. The air had the tang of early spring but was menaced by the threat of frost. The sky looked like a concave sheet of shiny black satin; there was a blindingly white moon, but it was hidden somewhere behind the grand pile from which she'd just emerged.

No going back, she was committed. She tiptoed down the stone steps and thought she heard a voice behind her. *Don't look back; if you do, you'll catch their eye and that'll be the end of your little foray!* She ignored it, pressing forward, and trying to tread more lightly across gravel until she reached the acoustic safety of stone paving, then walked smartly towards the end building of the west wing. Once round the corner, she paused in the shadow to get her breath, looked back to the lights of the Great Hall; nothing. Nobody in sight, except she thought she saw a flash come out of one of the unlit windows she'd just passed, as if there'd been someone in there communicating with whoever she'd thought she'd just heard behind her. It was as if there was a covert system of signalling going on.

She turned to face the way she must go and saw the next danger point, the tall arch to the estate offices courtyard – tall because coaches pulled by horses had once rode through there, then stabled and groomed by valets. Lorna moved, keeping clear of the pool of light which spilled through the arch, and peered round a stone column into the courtyard. It was deserted, and silent save for the low hum of an electric generator. She walked briskly across the rectangle of light and could see those tall windows which she and the others had walked past the previous evening. She could also see the almost imperceptible curve of stone which was the zodiac room. There was some satisfaction in knowing the whereabouts of that secret room. There was indeed undeniable strength in being in possession of a secret.

She could feel grass under her feet, as she hurried down a slight incline and onto the path which she knew would lead up to Cracklewood and the reservoir. As she walked clear of the buildings and into a landscape which looked no more than indefinable black smudges, it struck her that she hadn't given sufficient thought to planning this adventure. When she'd glanced at the visitor's map, it had looked easy. From the north side of the building, you just walked due east in a straight line. But the map showed no contours and already, in a matter of seconds, she had descended into what seemed to be a small ravine. The lights of the estate office courtyard less than a hundred yards behind her were hidden, and she was alone except for the sound of her footsteps, her breathing and the great murky outdoors.

Thank God for moonlight; it was sufficient to see the squat shape of a bridge, and she could feel the stone parapet, stingingly cold beneath her hand. She was crossing some kind of moat, but there was no shimmer of water from below, only a steep incline. She hadn't bargained for this and for just a moment she had to pause. Instead of silence; she could hear something breathing, over to her left. There was snuffling, grunting, and a moving shape. There was the silver thread of a wire fence, and beyond it the grubby but pale piebald skin of a pig. Of course! What self-respecting country estate would not have pigs?

Within a matter of seconds, she'd walked further up the hill, turned, and could once again see the lights of the house, but this time in the form of row after row of tiny rectangles of light. At last, she felt a fleeting satisfaction knowing that she could no longer be seen from the house, and it was then that she saw it. A figure standing at the corner of the west wing where she had paused to get her breath. It was silhouetted by light from the dozens of tiny windows. *Could it be clad in the grey of an immaculately tailored 1940s-style suit? It had to be him and he seemed to be looking straight at her.*

She'd considered looking for another less conspicuous exit from the house rather than the main one, but she had to accept the fact that in spite of the pioneering spirit she and her colleagues had demonstrated in escaping from the zodiac room, she hadn't got a clue as to the layout of the house, or the conditions outside which she might encounter. In that respect, there was no denying that she and her fellows *were* prisoners of a sort. She'd also been worried about bumping into one of the Bettys or, even worse, Spraycat himself. He'd probably been watching the front hall on CCTV from the warmth and security of his office. Well, so what? In another five minutes she would be speaking to Chas.

As she pressed on, she realised it was going to be more than five minutes, and certainly more than fifteen, before she was back at this point and walking home. It felt like holding your breath, being faced with having to do so for much longer than you thought, and feeling that you just can't do it. But she had to.

At first, she'd thought everything out here was totally silent. The last sounds she'd heard were the chomping of the pigs, but with some reluctance she had to admit that she was surrounded by a multitude of noises. Initially it seemed like that general rushing sound you get from a distant motorway. But as her hearing adjusted, there were eerie rustlings coming from the dark masses of foliage on either side of her. Tickings, crackings, slitherings, trillings and all manner of arpeggios were giving another dimension to the experience of being out of doors at night.

Most people didn't like Bartók. That's because they wanted a recognisable tune to hum. Lorna wasn't bothered about a tune; she wanted something different, even though she hadn't thought she was musical and had spent most of her life listening to pop music and musicals as a background to her work or play. She'd been surprised how captivated she'd been when one evening she'd heard Bartók's *The Night's Music*, and that's what these sounds reminded her of. But sitting in the soporific warmth of the Queen Elizabeth Hall on the South Bank was a far cry from stumbling up a hillside at 10.30 at night in late March and at least two hundred yards away from the nearest human.

But *was* she so far from others? Alright, she was plodding along in the dark in the middle of well over half a million acres. It was a private estate, but it wasn't gated or locked. Anybody could get in and wander. There was nothing to stop people driving through it, getting up to no good. Okay, if people tried camping, they would get reported by eagle-eyed woodsmen and receive short shrift from the estate's management. *But come on, Lorna!* The chances of there being somebody lurking nearby would be next to nothing. Statistically it would be far safer here than walking alone on Clapham Common, or strolling through Matching Thorpe for that matter, after 11.00 – particularly if there'd just been a darts match at the Bibber's Uproar.

She stopped again. Partly to get her breath, but mainly because she'd seen something she didn't understand. Over to her left and only just visible was the mouth of what looked like a tunnel. It was small; at least, had she been inclined to, she could have entered it without stooping, but not someone like Boone. The thought of even going any closer to it made her shudder. She could just make out the dull strands of what were probably rusted steel bars preventing anyone from getting in – or perhaps from getting out?

She tried to hurry, leaning forwards into the slope, but it was tough going. What she was walking on was only a path in the sense that others had been there before; in practice, it was no more than rough grass. As she struggled on upwards, the undergrowth either side of her was becoming less dense and what seemed to have formerly been undefinable dark voids she now recognised as pathways winding off in a number of directions. She stopped again. There was a hissing sound. Not like the white noise coming from stone vaulted chimneys over oak tables, but the kind of concentrated roar of quantities of water being forced through a tube or duct of some sort. She jumped. The hissing was making her even more nervous. Oh! To her left, there was a figure. She relaxed: it was a statue, and over to her right, another one. It seemed that as the ground began to level out, there was a network of woodland paths graced with the occasional stone figure, no doubt from classical mythology. A few steps further and she had reached the top.

The most spectacular thing was the light of the moon reflected in a body of water, the size of which seemed to Lorna to resemble one of the lesser lakes of the Lake District. It stretched as far as she could see. What showed on the visitor's map as a small clearing in the wooded summit was, to her overstimulated mind, immense.

As she walked closer to the reservoir's edge, the hiss became a roar, and to her horror she found herself gazing into the depths of a shaft spillway, a kind of giant plughole to drain off excess water. *Of course, that's what the tunnel was all about.* By the time the water had cascaded down the stepped sides of the gaping hole and run along a hundred yards or so of earth floor, it would have soaked away. Somewhere there would be a pump house to control the fountains in the lakes a hundred feet below. She noticed the edge of the reservoir was lined with what looked like stone, and it was bowl-shaped with a bullnosed overhanging edge. *God! If you fell in there, you'd never get out, and there's no handrail.*

Lorna took out her phone; yes, there was a signal! But she wouldn't be able to hear a thing with that racket going on, so she moved a few paces to where she had seen the shaded orangey-red and white of a lifebelt mounted on a wooden frame on the edge of the treeline. She tapped her phone; Chas wasn't answering. He would be driving back to Springhurst Hill from a naturalist's meeting in Loughton. Leave a message then; better still, a text: *Great course! Interesting and strange goings-on here with the management. Any chance of finding information on Golightly (the man) and Sir John Spreighmont? Could be a story? Love you! xxx*

She was just about to make her way back to the path when she thought she saw a red light over to her left. There was no doubt about it, a single red light, no more than a speck, and behind it; the distinct outline of a woodstore, or something like that – she could see the slope and the profile of each roof tile. There were no other lights, just blackness. The red light disappeared, and it seemed as if part of the woodshed had moved and separated itself from the main structure. At first, she thought the effect was caused by a tree bough blowing in the breeze; most of the trees were still in their winter skeletal form, but the air was perfectly still. As she inhaled, she could smell it – not woodsmoke, cigarette smoke. The implications of what she was doing suddenly hit her. If she had an accident out here, or something happened, it would be breakfast time before anyone noticed she was missing, and it would be her fault. She should not be here; she'd been warned, twice!

Lorna began walking towards the path. Walk! Don't run and don't look back. She quickened her pace, faster. Heart hammering. The urge to run was almost overwhelming. She was walking down the slope now, the winding paths to her left and right. She could glimpse the statues – no, it absolutely wasn't a statue. This was a real person. The noise of the hiss of the water running down the overspill was receding. There was no new sound behind her, no footsteps, but supposing he – she assumed it was a "he" – had sneaked into the woods. Any moment he could lunge out of the undergrowth, or simply appear yards in front of her – a ghostly, pale face, drained of life but full of malice. What had Trish told her only twenty-four hours ago? 'But please, *do* take extra care.' That bloody message was burning a hole in the pocket of her other chinos, and what was she doing? Taking risks.

She was walking so fast now she thought she might lose control of her leg movements. If she fell, he would get her. She could see the lights of the house in the distance. Faster! She turned – could no longer resist the urge. It was almost involuntary, a spasmodic lurch to her right. There was a face, it was him, in the mouth of the tunnel, behind the bars. But it wasn't the face of an aggressor; it was the visage of someone who was trapped, imprisoned, and not an adult, it was a child, a tiny child, a child so small it had not yet been born.

Lorna heard a cry. It was coming from her own body, and she was running now, sometimes slipping, slipping sideways, but somehow remaining upright. She reached the bridge, still running; she ran until she was leaning against the gatehouse wall of the estate offices. Leaning back, then forward, almost touching her toes and nearly puking. She looked back the way she'd come. There was nothing; it had all been in her mind. An innocent estate groundsman having a late cigarette. No doubt he would report her to Spraycat, but so what? She'd made contact with the outside world.

Back in her room, as Lorna tugged at the chest of drawers to barricade her door, she made the second big decision she'd made that day. When she returned to the reservoir the next evening to check her messages from Chas, maybe even speak to him, she would *not* do so alone. She had decided upon an ally.

10

The art of concealment requires, almost invariably and by definition, that they who wish not to be seen by an unwelcome party do not draw attention to themselves. Lorna need not have feared that her absence from the late evening chats might attract the scrutiny of others. Wednesday may have only been day three of the course, but the pace was quick, the activities intense, and the desire to sit late into the night speculating about the art and science of surveillance and the quirks of the administration was, it appeared, already on the wane.

Lorna and her new ally had agreed on a plan of convergence. It depended upon time to the nearest ten seconds so that neither would be seen loitering. They would both approach the Great Hall at a given time; if either overran, they would simply keep walking. The spaces were so vast and echoing that they would probably see or hear one another. Students occasionally opened the glazed front door and stood out on the stone-flagged "apron" to either enjoy the fresh air or to inhale tobacco, be it Virginia or perfumed vape. Boone was often to be seen there. Lorna had also decided upon the earlier time of 9.30; technically they would be leaving within the rules of the curfew, though her experiences of the previous evening had taught her that they were unlikely to return before 10.00.

Diane Vigianno.

'I don't think you'll need your label, Diane…'

'Force of habit.'

'Unless there's the odd woodsman you want to make the acquaintance of?'

Diane was struggling into her sand-coloured quilted anorak which she'd been carrying over her arm. She was wearing jeans of a similar hue. Perhaps not the ideal companion to go scaling a hundred-foot-high hill with, Diane had the appearance of someone who had reinvented themselves but not necessarily for the better, and by almost certainly changing shape over a period of years.

'I wasn't always big.'

But Lorna had been damned if she was going to make that journey alone. Diane had said she agreed with Lorna's comment "It's the way they look at you", and when at one of the breakout sessions Lorna had asked her whether she might fancy an outing into the estate at night, she'd said yes. For some reason, Lorna doubted that Diane would be phoning home.

This time Lorna had remembered her hacking jacket and beany hat. Quite probably the two of them resembled, to anybody who might have been watching, a pair of enlarged school pals as they strolled across the forecourt. Lorna was looking around, checking lighted windows which might contain prying eyes. Diane seemed to have no sense of urgency about their progress whatsoever and insisted on pausing right in the centre of the patch of light made by the arch leading to the estate office.

'Is that Betelgeuse?'

As Lorna urged Diane out of the limelight and into the shadows, two points struck her. No, it was not Betelgeuse, nor were there any stars visible because the sky was a mass of dingy cloud. Point two: unlike the previous evening, the air was claustrophobically warm. It was one of the eccentricities of England, the capriciousness of its weather. There was now almost certainly no need for the quilted anorak and certainly not for the hacking jacket. They had a hill to climb. As a consequence of the first point, an additional third concern was that there was no moon. It was going to be very dark indeed.

'Are there fish in the moat?'

'There isn't even any water, Diane.'

'What kind of pigs are they?' It was a fair question, particularly as Lorna had raised the subject in the first place. This time there was neither sound nor sight of the porkers.

Already it had taken them half an hour to get this far and, at the present rate, they wouldn't be back before 10.30. Whilst there was no urgency on time, it was making Lorna feel edgy.

'Is there a railway?'

'There're no trains here, Diane. It's so that excess water from the reservoir can soak away.'

Diane had insisted on stopping right at the mouth of the tunnel, and it was giving Lorna the creeps. It had also dawned on Lorna that the reason Diane had such a terse way of speaking was economy. She was carrying so much weight she had no excess energy to put into either speech or movement.

There were several more stops, including an alarming suggestion that they go and see one of the statues.

'Who are the statues of?' As they paused to rest, Diane actually furnished Lorna with a short description – perhaps long for Diane – of how she had visited Montreux and seen the statue of Freddie Mercury.

At long last, they reached the summit.

'Night's a good time for fishing.'

'Not here, Diane.'

This time, there was no moon reflected in the water; it just looked grey and dead.

Diane was completely unfazed by the noise or sight of the spillway shaft. She did not seem to share the primeval fear that Lorna experienced when staring down the black terraced edges of the giant plughole. To Lorna, it looked like the gullet of a colossal and hungry fish.

Lorna strode over to where the lifebelt was, took out her phone and called Chas. Again, no reply. She felt more than an annoyance this time. *He could be in the shower.* She glanced across at Diane, who was standing on one of those painstakingly made edging stones and barely two metres from the mouth of the spillway shaft. Her shoulders were heaving up and down, and for one chilling moment Lorna thought she was weeping – that is until she became aware that Diane was trying to get her breath back after that infernally slow climb, her body rocking backwards and forwards as she tried to absorb the air which was hanging over the lake.

Lorna felt a degree of unease, but she was reading Chas's reply to yesterday's text. *Golightly ex-MI5, nothing on Spreighmont yet, will keep trying.* Well done, Chas! There was a slight irony. She was just about to tap in a reply when she sensed a movement. Entering the right corner of her eye, travelling at something that might be likened to the speed of a shooting star, it streaked off stage left. It could have been a bat, a missile, or just her own wild imagination. When Lorna looked up, Diane was gone.

For an unaccountable interval, Lorna just stood gaping at the place where Diane had been standing. She rushed to the spot, looked at the water. It was still grey; no light, no reflection, no sign of movement. She dropped on all fours, then to the prone position. Bubbles? Nothing, and that Christ-awful infernal racket! Lorna got up, ran, first one way, then another direction.

'Diane!'

Nothing except the hiss.

'Diane! For Christ's sake, where are you?'

She blundered into undergrowth, still shouting. She turned; the lifebelt? Slogged over to its housing, released it, dragged by its dangling ropes, and hurled into the water in the vain hope that Diane might surface and grab it. There was nothing. Lorna was leaning forward, hands gripping her knees while she bellowed into the din and the night. The woodsman?

She lurched towards the woodstore, staggering as she tripped in the darkness. Fumbling for the door, found, but wouldn't open. It was just a store, there was nobody, and she was alone. She would have to leave the scene and seek help elsewhere.

At first, she was jogging, sobbing, coughing, breathing spasmodically. The incline of the hill was carrying her faster, faster until she lost control and fell almost head over heels. She kicked out, stamped into a vertical position and began running again. She stopped, leant forward, spewing, and as she lifted her eyes, she could see the mouth of the tunnel. There was a face; it was different from the awful phantasm of yesterday. The face was connected to a body clad in a sand-coloured quilted anorak.

Lorna was still running as she crashed over the gravel of the forecourt. There was a figure standing at the bottom of the stone steps leading up to the glass doors. It was dressed in a grey, immaculately tailored 1940s cut suit, the face adorned with a moustache. Lorna could feel herself leave the ground as she hurled herself at it. One of her fists had closed round the edge of the hand-stitched lapels, the other was grasping the man's right ear.

'You fucking bastard!' She was stamping, stamping on those fucking steel-tipped Oxfords. She was fucking stamping and fucking punching. Could feel his silk tie, she was pulling, pulling tight. 'There was no need to kill her!' Lorna could feel her arms abruptly pulled away from her target; she heard the squeak of leather, felt the force of strong arms grip her from behind. She shut her eyes.

Her fists were still pummelling the air as she felt herself lifted by hands, arms – how many pairs? Two, three, four? She could smell hessian or something. She was lying face down, could feel it pressing against her nose, hands securing her arms, legs, her back. Her body was slipping as it was being carried, sloping, but the hands were securing her to whatever surface she was now lying on, so she didn't slide off. She was twisting; first one way, then the other. Then there was leather behind her back, under her buttocks, her mouth could feel the coolness of something – a drinking glass? – something liquid, her head being pulled back. It felt good and she realised she was parched beyond belief. It was bitter, gritty, and it made her cough.

*

The hands of the clock said seven. It was one of those type of clocks she remembered they used to have in schools, with big flat hands and roundy Arabic numerals, black on white with the second hand in bright red. Red to match the lips of Elaine Wayfarer, who was standing looking at Lorna. Except it wasn't Elaine. There was exactly the same grey three-quarter length suit, cream shirt, *pale* stockings this time – and no doubt cream garter belt encasing those youthful pale hips beneath. There were black patent shoes, but the hair was different – same circa 1948 style, but it was red, paleish red, what some people liked to call strawberry blonde. Somehow it didn't look right. Grey suits don't look right with blondes – remember Kim Novak in Hitchcock's *Vertigo*? – and they look even odder with strawberry blondes. It was definitely a different girl.

'I'm Rita – Ellcock, the night receptionist. It's seven o'clock.'

'I can see that.'

'I'll bring you some coffee.'

'Listen! I have to leave.'

'Yes, we'll talk about that.'

The girl left the room. She knew how to move better than Elaine. This was going to be fun.

The room Lorna had been sleeping in, full-length on a sofa and under a blanket, was next to the breakout room. It was a kind of office, but Lorna already knew that. She'd had a good look around when she'd awoken at five and groped around in a still groggy state trying to find some kind of toilet. She'd seen the red-lipped strawberry-haired "beauty" fast asleep in a nearby armchair. She'd noticed that the office, and other rooms she'd explored, also had mirrored wall panelling. The breakout room, it seemed, was a kind of goldfish tank that could be observed from practically all angles and 24/7. But then she, and other people – students, that is – had already spotted that. Including Diane.

'How are you feeling?' Strawberry returned with the coffee.

'Well enough to go home.'

'I'm very sorry to have to tell you that your friend is dead.'

'I believe I told you that.'

'Please excuse me one moment.'

The girl again left the room, leaving the door ajar. Lorna could hear a soft knock on the door of another adjacent room, heard that door close. No doubt she was now talking to Spreighmont and checking up on how much she could reveal. No doubt, Spreighmont was also watching Lorna, every sip of coffee, every expression, every move. The girl returned.

'You did tell us that, but your friend did not fall down the spillway shaft as you had said.'

Lorna must have been babbling; whether that was before she was given the sedative or after, she couldn't be sure… And why was it "your friend"?

'We're talking about Diane?'

There was another pause, but this time the girl decided to reply without a prompt from next door.

'The other student who went with you up to Cracklewood Reservoir.' If they didn't want to say her name then that was up to them. 'The divers found the body in the water close to the spillway overflow.'

'Divers?' That suddenly made the situation seem more real.

'The body's been taken to the hospital. There has to be a post-mortem. The police have questioned the staff here.'

The police! Lorna could feel her heart starting to hammer. The sedative must have well and truly worn off.

'The students will be told in their individual course sessions at 10.00. They'll only be told the basics to avoid any rumour, and what the police have revealed to us. They – the police, that is – will probably call on you at your home.'

'Can I use the office phone to speak to my partner.' It was a demand, not a question. Of course, Spreighmont would be listening to every word.

'Of course.'

'Chas?'

'Lorna, I'm sorry we didn't get to speak before. I am trying.'

Oh, his digging information on the management – she'd almost forgotten. His voice sounded shaky. She was the one who was supposed to be shaky.

'Look, love, something's happened here, I've got to go home—'

'What? Are you okay? Are you hurt?'

'No, I'm okay. There's been an accident. I was involved – at least, I'm a witness, but it's been too much of a shock. Continuing with the course is a no go, I'm afraid.'

'I'll come and pick you up. Come and stay with me at Springhurst.'

Why? Of course, he didn't know the details, but why was he in such a hurry to drive up here, pick her up and take her back to Springhurst?

'Springhurst Hill? No, I need to go home. Chas, I don't need picking up.' She needed time to think.

'It sounds as if you've had a shock, I'll look after you – for a few days.'

'That's lovely of you, but I have to be at home. When I've had time to calm down and think, I'll ring you and tell you what's happened.'

'I'll meet you off the train then, at Welwyn, and we can talk then.'

'Chas. I really don't need meeting at Welwyn.'

'I'll meet you at Harlow then.'

'Okay, okay! If you insist!' God! Couldn't he get it? She'd had an upset, she needed to be on her own. She'd given in to him, but she wasn't going to Springhurst with him. He'd take her to Matching, she'd explain to him what had happened as best she could, then he'd drive back to Springhurst. She was wishing she'd decided not to ring him in the first place, but she'd just felt she had to let somebody else know what was happening. She couldn't bring herself to tell him someone had died and she'd been involved, not just yet.

'Text me time of arrival when you change at Welwyn.'

'When I know it and I've got a signal. And we'll take it from there.'

'Love you!'

'Yes, love you too!' She disconnected.

The girl returned. No doubt she'd heard the details as well.

'I'm going off duty now. Elaine's due in at eight; she'll run you to the station.'

11

The car journey from Golightly to the railway station had been made in total silence. Lorna's luggage had arrived – almost diabolically – in the office. Someone else had done her packing. The leathery Blogg had appeared to help carry – not *down* this time, but *up* a flight of steps. Lorna was being removed by a side door leading up from the basement where she had spent the night in one of the subterranean office rooms. Elaine Wayfarer had arrived, as Rita had forecast, at 8.00 and – perhaps as a mark of respect for the dead – minus her red lips. Lorna, in a state of ironic observation and under close escort by Wayfarer, was surprised that for her cloak-and-dagger exit from basement up to Elaine's car, the management had not placed a blanket over her head.

As Elaine had slowed the car to negotiate the gatehouses in the fake battlemented walls, Lorna had thought that the stone had acquired a sickly greenish tinge like a never-before-seen rock face being observed from inside a space capsule, or a deep-sea probe at the bottom of the Mariana Trench. It just hadn't been possible that she had ever thought that it looked like candy.

At the station, Elaine had accompanied Lorna onto the platform, had waited with her until the train arrived, and not left until it was drawing out of the station with Lorna firmly in her seat, her face mask securely over her mouth. They did not wave at one another.

Once in motion on the 8.50, Lorna took out her phone to text Chas with the time of arrival at Harlow, noticed the message icon, and opened it to find that it was from the "enquiry office" at Golightly to Chas giving the train arrival details at Harlow. Lorna had merely been copied in. It would appear that her status in this matter had been reduced from participant to observer. Of course, Golightly had the details of next of kin of all their students; this was no more than emergency protocol.

She was about to look at her newsfeed when she saw another pull-down message icon.

How was Golightly? Write a review!

'Fuck you!' she bawled through her mask to a far from empty railway carriage and threw the phone into her bag.

'Tickets please, luv!' said a cheery voice close to her ear.

12

She'd known something was wrong from the start. I mean, *really* wrong. Chas's face!

He was standing on the station platform. Was it that she just wasn't taking this thing seriously enough? Her course was ruined. She had been responsible – to some degree, indirectly, partly – for the death of one of her fellow students. It had been unwise for her to ask Diane to go with her up to the reservoir – it could even be seen as a form of coercion. Although a late-night walk on the estate wasn't breaking the law, it *was* going against house rules, and Golightly – like it or not – was also to some degree responsible for the health and welfare of its visitors, guests, students, and its word should therefore have been obeyed. Had Lorna not asked Diane to come with her, Diane would almost certainly still be alive, and probably happily – though, in reality, perhaps more laconically – still transcendentally meditating. The post-mortem, the inquest – oh God! – if there *had* to be one, would clarify all. But for Christ's sake, Chas! Did he have to look like the nuclear holocaust had happened? She wasn't going to go to prison. Just *what* had *they* told him?

And there was the way he'd held her, when they were standing on the platform, several thousand nanoseconds longer than he'd ever done when she'd been away before. When they'd got into his car, he'd sat there at first, trying to smile. Then he started driving. The car had to crawl out of Harlow, as for part of the way they were following an anti-vax demonstration.

'Chas, why are we still on the A414?'

'To get to the M11.'

But, Chas, we're not going to Springhurst Hill.' He still didn't get it. 'We cross the M11 at Matching Green; we're not going on it now. What's wrong with the B183?'

Just before the junction with the M11, there's a layby. Why he chose to stop in that Godforsaken place to tell her, she couldn't imagine. He just didn't know what to do and, under the circumstances, in retrospect, quite understandable. There were no other vehicles in the lay-by. He pulled up among the usual sea of crisp packets, fragments of polystyrene, dusty grey molehills and termitaria formed where people had emptied the contents of their ashtrays onto pitted tarmac.

'Chas, I just want to go to my house. Can we do that?'

'I've been there.'

There? No need for him to sound so cryptic.

'Where?'

'Your house.' His voice was soft and breathy.

'Yes?' Lorna could feel time slowing. Getting slower and slower.

'I've been there since seven o'clock this morning.'

Lorna's eye fixed on a tangle of wire coat hangers, inexplicably abandoned, perhaps by the same person who had been responsible for arranging a suite of furniture consisting of a sofa, a dining table, an armchair (minus its seat cushion) and a dark wood wardrobe. The ensemble stood on the tarmac, exactly as it might have done in some bedsit, but minus the walls of the room.

'What are you saying, Chas?'

'I thought – well, I'd hoped you wouldn't, that's why I wanted to come and collect you – that you might have seen it on the news?'

'No, Chas, I haven't looked at my phone apart from to send you a text.'

This was going to be like getting blood out of a stone. It couldn't be a flood, a tornado? An explosion?

An F35 Lightning stealth fighter from RAF Marham crashing into it? A fire, that was the most likely.

'Has there been a fire, Chas?'

There was a pause.

'A fire, Chas. Has there been a fire?'

'… A sinkhole.'

Images were flashing through Lorna's mind. The spillway shaft, the sensation of movement in the air she'd experienced at the moment Diane had vanished, and standing outside her bedroom door at Golightly with Trish – "Do take *extra* care".

'When did it happen?'

'About ten o'clock last night—'

'Can you be more specific?' she snapped. 'I need to know, precisely.'

'The police told me ten.'

'The police?'

'I spoke to them this morning: the police, the gas supplier, the electric, the water services… on the site.'

"*The site*". So that was it, it was no longer a house, a home, it was a site.

'You were there?'

'I told you! I've been there all morning. I saw pictures of it posted on somebody's Twitter page, for God's sake, this morning at six o'clock! I recognised it, drove straight up. I haven't been back to Springhurst. I've talked to everybody I can who might be of practical help, but there's nothing more I can do. I was just about to ring you when you rang me.'

Lorna studied the pathetic ensemble of furniture

outside the car window. Objects which might seem pointless now, but at least they were real. What Chas was telling her was unreal. Once, someone had arranged these objects with pride, they had admired them, quite possibly shown them and shared them with friends, looked forward to curling up on that sofa, perhaps even made love on it. Looking closer at the furniture pathos, Lorna could see that either there in that lay-by, or perhaps elsewhere, someone, or something, had attempted to set fire to it.

Chas didn't speak, probably didn't know what to say. They sat; she listening to the roar of traffic on the highway. That was pointless as well, car after swishing car. Most of them with just one person in. They couldn't all be going to or from work, going shopping, doing business, or hurrying to visit a relative. She'd seen this stretch of road practically deserted throughout lockdowns. What were the drivers of these private cars doing during lockdown? Sitting on sofas like the one she was gazing at? Perhaps she should be grateful to be able to see a non-stop procession of cars; it was a sign that Britain was back in business, the life blood of commerce once again flowing.

'Chas, we have to go there, now!'

'Lorna, do you understand what's happened?'

'Yes, I do. I'm sorry, Chas, but, I have to go and see for myself.'

There was no point in explaining it to Chas, but Lorna did know a little about bereavement. Perhaps Chas did, but if so, he'd never mentioned the death of his own parents – if indeed they were dead. It was a subject he seemed not prepared to shed the faintest glimmer of light on and Lorna had always felt she was trespassing to even ask. And make no mistake, the sudden forced and involuntary removal of one's home *is* a form of bereavement.

She'd looked after both her parents prior to their premature deaths. When Mum died, she was too busy helping Dad to do much grieving. It was when Dad died that it hit her, and the real hammer blow was the realisation of what nobody ever tells you about your parents dying – the simple fact that you've never known a time when they weren't there. You're into totally unchartered emotional territory and, with no sibling with which to share or compare, you're on your own. No matter how much you might intellectualise the event, you can never be emotionally prepared. When Mum had died, she'd not gone to see her body in the chapel of rest – Dad had gone on his own. She'd had dreams about Mum after that, about Mum coming back from the dead, so when Dad died, she'd made sure that she went to the chapel to see his body. It was a simple ritual of closure. It meant that she would see for herself that he was dead – as if it were the reverse situation of the garden of Gethsemane, not "he is risen" but stark staring proof that he is dead, and with it the release of being able to move on. It almost seemed like a blasphemous thought that there should be any comparison between the death of a close relative and losing one's home. But Lorna knew there was and that if there was going to be any chance of her moving on, then she must go and witness the catastrophe for herself. There was also the never spoken of but indelible experience of the death of an unborn child for her still to deal with.

She turned to Chas. He seemed to be contemplating the driving wheel. When he looked at her, it was as if he was somehow apologising that he hadn't managed the situation better.

'Chas, I know you're trying to be very practical and straight about all this, but something truly odd is happening.'

What time it took place *was* important, because, strange as it might seem, it appeared to Lorna that Diane falling in the reservoir and Lorna's house falling into the sinkhole were both part of the same event.

'Lorna, do you see?' Chas sounded almost pleading. 'If you had been in the house, you would have been killed. Being on the course saved you!'

13

What *does* it feel like to lose one's home? Some might well take the view that a high-flying marketing executive who retired at fifty-five on a substantial salary with a fat pension pot should easily be able to take an event like that on the chin. It's an insurance claim, *so get over it, will you!* As Lorna soon discovered, though folk who found that they were living next to a sinkhole could do nothing to prevent the value of their property sinking to zero, should the actual *fabric* of the house be damaged, then they could claim. Lorna's house hadn't just been damaged, it had effectively disappeared and was little more than a spoil of smashed timber, clay, steel, stone, concrete, glass and plaster; builders' rubble melded with soft fabrics, plastics, paper, once-edible food and organic plants. All had been deposited at the bottom of an almost perfect hole measuring ten metres in diameter. To make matters worse – or perhaps less complicated – the heavy cloud of the previous evening had drifted south, and much of east Anglia was experiencing steady rainfall. It was as if a giant food mixer had been crammed full of rough chopped organic matter, chugged its way round no more than a couple of abrupt revolutions and had water added. Nothing was salvageable; it was a nightmarish inedible gazpacho.

To Lorna, that might be *one* way of looking at it – perhaps the estate agent's view, or, for that matter, the insurer and their underwriters, another. But what does it actually *feel* like? Because millions of people in the third world experienced that feeling *every* day as a result of natural causes or war. That is, those of them who were fortunate enough to even have a home in the first place – more specifically, according to what Lorna had read, only seven per cent of the world's population actually had their own home. Millions of folks evicted every day throughout the world might well have broken rules, transgressed laws, but that didn't mean they didn't feel the heartbreak of being separated from their home – or having their home destroyed.

House and home had interlocking meaning for Lorna. The structure was inseparable from the emotional dependence it created. She saw it as a pathological need; like a baby doesn't merely take nourishment from its mother's breast or a bottle – it's an instinctive need for comfort. You lived, you loved, and you learnt in a home. You ventured out every day to stretch yourself in the world, but you returned every evening to refresh, rejuvenate, and to reinvent yourself ready for the next day. To lose that in one fell swoop was to Lorna a trauma of a seriousness which wasn't easily quantifiable.

House and home were to Lorna as a studio is to an artist, or a laboratory is to a scientist. They were not just an opportunity for self-expression, experiment or human development, they were a necessity, an essential. No matter how meagre the possessions it contained, or how unfashionable or tasteless the furniture might appear to others, house and home were a life blood, and for that to be taken away meant that a person no longer had a life.

Lorna's mother had been proud of her terraced house in Dagenham and having to leave it had been an emotional wrench. But her parents had welcomed being rehoused. What they were given provided infinitely more comfort and convenience to what they were leaving behind. Lorna could testify that the sanctimonious social scientist's argument that they had been condemned to a life of concrete by some beknighted and ogreish architect simply wasn't true.

Lorna had bought what became her first and only house, way beyond her financial means, by letting rooms. Like millions of others of her age group, she'd spent hours at parties talking about surges in house values, but that didn't mean that it didn't have an emotional value to her. As she became more financially able, she depended less on tenants and for the last fifteen years she'd been there on her own. She and Chas had never lived there together – in fact, they'd never lived anywhere together.

Her plight that morning was nothing compared to the trillions of refugees there'd been in the history of the world, but it was the nearest thing she could imagine to being a refugee. Of course, many refugees hadn't just lost their homes, they'd had their loved ones killed – sometimes right in front of them. It was unthinkable, nevertheless it made her think of Diane. Diane was hardly a loved one, loved ones are our responsibility, but Diane had been, in *some way*, Lorna's responsibility. She was feeling that this morning's loss on top of last night's loss was very hard indeed. Which made it even more difficult to bear as Chas drove into Matching Thorpe and she could see the thousands of cars which had invaded this rural village which had been her home for the last twenty-five years.

'I'm truly sorry, Lorna. I didn't want you to see this. They've been arriving all morning. It's on social media and everybody's newsfeeds. They just can't keep away.'

Every inch of the street was parked up with cars, every tuft of every grass verge was nose to tail with MPVs and SUVs. The nearer Chas's car came to Lorna's house, the more people there were streaming along road and common. Many seemed to have cockapoos and labradoodles on leads. Some of them were in groups, strung out across the road. One group of white quilt-coated and panel-hatted individuals had linked arms as if taking part in some ancient folk ceremony. Not one was wearing a face mask.

'Hoot!' shouted Lorna, as Chas slowed almost to a halt. The group reluctantly broke and scattered, one of them raising two fingers. Lorna couldn't actually see it, but she could feel the vibrations. Somewhere somebody was bouncing a football on the road's tarmacked surface.

The overnight rain had stopped and there was a weedy glimmer of sun. The hawthorn blossom of her beloved hedge – early this year – the gates with their aqua-painted spears of wood, the pond, the cherry trees, the market garden and the polytunnel which contained her small, and undeniably unsustainable, swimming pool; her Golf cabriolet convertible sitting on the brick-paved hardstanding. They were all there. From the inside of Chas's car, the view seemed normal, but for three differences.

One: it was restricted to glimpses through the gaps of an almost continuous line of parked cars and a press of people; Lorna could hear and feel the bump, bump of hands and elbows against the windows of the car. Chas edged through at a snail's pace. There was the source of the football sound: a ginger-haired man, his large pink-dungareed partner, and a fat ginger child.

The rhythm was slow, unhurried, deliberate, and Lorna couldn't decide whether it might be suitable as percussive funereal accompaniment to *Raise Me Up* by Westlife or *Lay Me Down* by Sam Smith.

Difference number two: the gates were standing open, and yellow and black tape was stretched across the opening. The third and oddest difference was that the familiar two-storey gabled, white rendered and weatherboarded house with its trellised porch, wisteria and terracotta pots was gone.

There were two police standing by the gate – man and woman. Both were wearing face masks, but they seemed to be the only ones who were.

'They're not even regular police, they're community support!'

'I'll try and park round the back on the service lane – that's where I was this morning.'

But it was the same story; a continuous chain of cars parked, half on the worn gravel track and half on rough grass. In the short interval it had taken Chas to go and pick Lorna up at Harlow, he had lost his valuable parking space near the house. Like the front, the gate was wide open, but no hazard tape. Two men in hi-vis clothing and holding steel bars had prised open the water inspection cover. This time there was one PCSO standing outside the gate. Lorna wound down her window.

'I'm the owner—'

'I can't let you in.'

'We just want to park—'

'That's all anybody wants to do.'
'We have to look at the house—'
'I'm sorry, you can't park here.'
'Everybody else has—'
'It's full – sorry, lav, it's chaos—'
'Why aren't there more police?'
'We're short-staffed; everybody's self-isolating and there's an anti-vax demo in Harlow.'
'Yes, we've seen it.'

They had to join the end of the tail of parked cars which stretched from the house, through Matching, and across the common.

'Haven't you seen enough?'
'I have to get a bit nearer.'

As they walked back to the house, they passed a van selling coffee and hot dogs and other squelchy-looking twenty-first century comfort fodder. There was the continuous sound of pop music and the steady thump of drum and bass. A man wandered about through the crowds blowing on something that looked like a whistle. He had a tray held on string round his neck. There were coloured whistles in his tray. As Chas and Lorna fought their way through the throng, Lorna could hear the cheery sound of birdsong coming from the man's whistle. There was an atmosphere of carnival and a different kind of thump, the sort of sound that causes a physical tremor in the earth and, like the aftershock of a seismic event, goes right through you; it was the repetitive tremor of a football being bounced on tarmac.

Lorna could overhear snatches of conversation from onlookers.

'Was it an explosion?' asked one voice.

'Did it explode?' asked a second.

'What's the difference?' a third voice wanted to know.

'Was the destruction caused by an explosion or did the destruction cause an explosion?' repeated the first.

'For God's sake!' shouted Lorna, as Chas held onto her arm. 'That's my home you're talking about.'

'Yes, but we need to know,' bellowed the first voice. 'It's in the public interest!'

Fights, road accidents, explosions, public suicides and the possibility of terminal illness of folk in the public eye – in particular media stars – people displayed a morbid fascination of all of them. Andy Warhol had known of the value of these things for years; he'd spotted their potential as saleable commodities, art – he'd seen "beauty" in the San Quentin electric chair. Excitement, violence, death – there was no demarcation between these and beauty. A fact of which Lorna, as a person with a thirty-year career in marketing, was brutally aware. There was no escape in claiming that just because she was the owner it made her exempt from being a gawper at someone else's misfortune.

Lorna thought that it might look to Chas as if she was persisting in a hopeless situation. Why on earth was she putting herself through all this? She could see he was torn between telling people to go home, barracking the police into making them leave, and offering comfort to Lorna in this strange bereavement.

They reached the front gate of the house.

'I'm the owner.'

The female PCSO seemed to take charge. 'We can't let you in.'

'I just want to see if there's anything I can do—'

'The site's all been made safe; electric, gas, water… hey!'

The large man and woman – he with a ginger forked beard and wearing a bright blue panel hat; she dressed in pink dungarees and with a body mass index of at least thirty-two – had waddled through the hazard tape; others followed, some children, one fattish with ginger hair and a red face. The boy with the football under his arm.

It was the first clear view Lorna had had of the crater. Its edges dark, a tangle of plant roots, and at its centre a pool of brilliant white light on the still water as the sun broke free of the cloud. Lorna could see no identifiable items in the crater, it was just mush – except one. Somehow, a paper photograph had squeezed itself out of the small golden frame which had once contained it. No one else would know what it was of, but Lorna did. It was of her, her mother and Matt at Brightlingsea lido taken thirty-four years ago when Matt was four, taken by Dad. It was floating face upwards.

The ginger man was clowning on the edge, pretending to fall backwards into the cavity and stretching out his arms in histrionic pose, his pink-dungareed partner clinging to him and whooping, while the red-faced child held out the selfie stick with one hand, the other hand holding the football.

'Cheeeese!'

'I'm asking you to leave, now!' The male PCSO had approached them.

'Alright, alright!' remonstrated Ginger Forkie, as if the copper was being the biggest spoilsport in the world.

'You should be ashamed of yourselves!' Lorna could feel Chas's arm gripping hers.

'What do yow know about it?' mouthed the pink one in powerful west-midlands brogue. 'It's awnly a bit of fon for the babby! Have yow got keeds?'

Lorna was speechless.

'Oi though not.'

'Come on, Courtney!' urged Ginger Forkie.

'Ignore her, Lorna, she's just fat wap,' whispered Chas.

As the pink woman pushed past, she thrust her unmasked face close and Lorna could see the glassiness of tiny, computer-gaming, unseeing eyes. Lorna could feel the porcine nose. She could smell the burgered and barbequed breath, and watched almost mesmerised as the wide, white, greasy knob of a chin wobbled up and down.

'Yow, wench, iv got a seriuss coise of selfie-envy. Yow needs to grow oop.'

14

There was nothing else for it but for Lorna to go with Chas to his apartment in Springhurst Hill. The ensuing days – not to mention weeks – were going to be full of activity for her.

She had already spoken to her insurers, who had confirmed that as the house had been totally destroyed, it would be a full claim to the market value – at the time of the incident – of the property, including the land, and any further remedial works which might be required to make the site safe, any salvage work, plus demolition of adjacent buildings which might be required to provide a safe and levelled building site either for her to rebuild on, or for resale. It was not made clear – as things stood at present – as to any future insurances of new buildings which might be built on that site. She was assuming that she was also covered for either temporary rental during a period of reconstruction, or over the interval which might be required until she purchased a new property, though this was not clear either in the documents or via the insurer's agent.

Lorna's gut feeling was to move elsewhere, to flee the awful memory. Chas agreed and was already suggesting that she stay with him – at least for a period, until she found her feet. But as Chas drove south down the M11, a further feeling overcame Lorna. Though offering a refuge from her misfortune, the solution seemed to also threaten the independence she most valued. Losing one's home is like having one's identity removed. Would it strengthen their relationship or would it stifle it? She had suffered bereavement, it was a triple – no, quadruple – bereavement; i) on a fairly mundane level, her creative writing course had been wrecked, ii) she had helplessly watched the death of one of her coursemates, a death which would not have occurred at that moment had she acted differently, iii) she had had her house and home totally destroyed, and as a result, iv) had lost – at least temporarily – her independence. There was no denying the enormity of this; there was also no denying that these – or similar – experiences were suffered in part, or all, by millions of people, in various ways, across the world every day! That feeling alone weighed heavily upon her, it was almost as if Lorna was entering – falling – into a kind of imprisonment. She would deal with it, would treat it like a professional project – a marketing account or an assignment. But she also had – from the time only three days ago that she had spoken to Trish Westfall, her colleague on the course, that unlikely spiritual medium – an inkling that she was setting foot into a state of illness.

Chas's emotional credentials on house and home were different from Lorna's. If asked to put her finger on exactly where the difference lay, Lorna would have to admit she would not be able to define it. He ticked the same basic boxes of the ideas of retreat, rejuvenation, and self-expression as Lorna, but there was some difference in fundamentals. Lorna had stayed in the same house for twenty-five years, whereas during the same period Chas had moved five times. A divorce accounted for one move, ten years since. He said he had no children. Maybe the difference lay merely in the fact that he was male, though that did seem a little unfair as a criterion for analysis.

Matching Thorpe is decidedly Essex country village; Springhurst Hill – though Chas was always insisting "it's a town" – is unequivocally suburban – suburban to what? Suburban to London, and that was Chas. The two of them were both "London", she Dagenham, he Tottenham – so he was always claiming – though at times Lorna thought he sounded just like a scouser. But Chas was a mimic; he could do Russian even though he couldn't speak a word.

Though via her parents Lorna had taken to the country, Chas, it seemed, had remained "London". His was an apartment, the whole of the ground floor of a rambling, tall-gabled, pinkish brick Victorian house. The first-floor flat hadn't appealed to Chas, even though it had better views. The ground floor had an extensive cellar for workshops and storage, and, best of all, majority access to the sizeable garden. There was also a generous front garden, though like most such areas in Britain it had fallen to hardstanding for the inevitable two, three, or even four cars which were all part of the now forty million – so Chas was always saying – car population of the UK.

There was a deep porch extending within the basic footprint of the house; it had patterned blue, red, and green tiles contemporary with the 1870-ish building. It was from that porch that Lorna first saw two police entering through the front gate. Yes, police. Bizzies, as Chas sometimes cryptically referred to them. She'd seen the marked car parked on the opposite side of the road as Chas had turned into the driveway.

'Hello! Lorna Collins?'

'Yes.'

'Police. We're sorry to bother you, but we'd like to have a short chat with you about the events at Golightly last night. It's nothing to worry about – it's information *for* you, rather than the other way round. It shouldn't take more than five minutes.'

It was a man and a woman. She was doing the talking – perhaps woman to woman, rather than seniority? He'd been sitting in the driver's seat.

'Fine. Can they come in?' Lorna was speaking to Chas. 'This is my partner, Chas Peake. It's his apartment, but you obviously know that already.'

'… Depends. How are you feeling, Lorna?' And to the policewoman, 'Is this going to help or harm?'

'It should help.'

'I'll get the luggage in; you take them in the front, it's more private.'

'I don't want private, Chas. We can all sit in the kitchen – if that's okay with you.' Already she was bringing *her* business into *his* home. Could that be a sign of things to come?

As the man came near, she could smell he was a smoker; he was chewing but trying to conceal it. A point struck her. These were local police, they knew where to come, but how did they know Lorna would be at Chas's or when? They must have taken note of the disaster at Matching Thorpe and assumed that this is where she'd be.

Chas offered the police seats on one of the two sofas which stood either side of the doors opening out onto the garden. He and Lorna took the other. Chas perched on the edge; she leant back, almost felt relaxed. Not too relaxed, she hoped. The man glanced up the garden, looked as if he wanted to comment on their surroundings, thought otherwise. The woman spoke.

'The student who died, who you were with last night, the hospital has confirmed that her identity is different to the one she was using.'

Lorna gave a half cough, half laugh. It was one of those mannerisms delivered by people who have had their patience tried over a number of occasions, expressing irony, or perhaps simply asking, "Can this get any weirder?". It was also, she imagined, perhaps a little more defensive than she might have intended.

'According to information we've received from the hospital, and…' – there was a slight pause – 'and Golightly administration office, this person has been identified not as Diane Vigianno, as listed on the student register, but someone called Stacey Albarn.'

Lorna could feel the woman looking at her closely.

'Do you know anybody by that name, and, if so, can you think of any reason why she should wish to conceal her identity?'

'No.' Even as she said it, Lorna experienced a kind of ethereal rush in her brain: '*Cop hold of this, Stace!*' Then it was gone.

'That's fine then.'

'What about cause of death? As the last person to see her, I feel confused, puzzled and upset.' Was that the right reply?

'Autopsy – post-mortem – two to three days, perhaps sooner. We'll let you know.'

'Who, then, *is* Diane Vigianno?'

'She *does* exist.' Was that the nearest police got to a joke? It almost felt like one. 'Diane has been traced and informed. Stacey's next of kin are being notified right now.'

'Will there be an inquest?'

'That depends on the result of the post-mortem. If the coroner is satisfied that there are no suspicious circumstances, then probably no. However, even if a coroner releases the body for burial or cremation, they are still at liberty to call an inquest if they're not totally satisfied.'

'Why? I mean, why the deception?'

'I can't tell you. That's why we need to talk to Diane. Until then, we can only speculate, as you also can, but as I said when we were outside, it's probably nothing to worry about. I *can* tell you that Diane had a work assignment abroad, so any of us can assume from that that she wasn't able to attend the course. That's perhaps where Stacey came in as a substitute, all quite innocent, and pretending to be someone you're not isn't against the law – unless you obtain money or goods – but as we can see, it can lead to complications if there's a fatality. As I say, we'll be in touch about the post-mortem result.'

15

The insurance brokers had been in touch. It was Jason and he was using phrases like "straightforward", "plain sailing", and "We're gearing up". *Let's hope so*, thought Lorna. She'd worked in marketing for thirty-five years; she knew it was all about wheel-oiling and schmoozing. People in third world countries lost their savings, livelihoods and homes every day on a mind-blowing scale. The places and the people in the world who most needed insurance couldn't afford the premiums. Yet they all seemed to have mobile phones. You saw them almost daily on the news – bereft of everything; home, possessions, and perhaps filmed somewhere in Southeast Asia, marooned and perched on the only visible remaining morsel of dry land in square miles, or in war-torn zones squatting in refugee camps, yet still jabbing at their mobile phones. With infrastructure destroyed, where did they charge them? Even rough sleepers all seemed to have mobile phones.

Houses falling into sinkholes in Britain was a relatively rare occurrence, but whole villages being swept away by floods in Southeast Asia wasn't. Catastrophes like these were not only common, they were becoming widespread, and as sixty per cent of the world's 7.8 billion population lived in Asia, they were a threat to most people in the world. But attitudes were changing. Chas said that the age of anno virus had exposed to a hitherto ignorant public: i) Britain would no longer be protected by the Gulf Stream and before so long could expect winters reaching twenty degrees below zero. ii) Sea levels were rising – yes, even around Britain, which in the non-too-distant future could expect mass erosion of coastal land and the reappearance of inland salt water lakes. iii) World ground aquifers were half empty after steadily pumping water since their discovery in the 1940s to grow supplies of tomatoes, coffee beans – you name it! iv) Viruses were a threat in the form of, at worst, mass death – even if it didn't say so in the press every day – and at least daily mass absences from work through self-isolation. v) The number of cars on UK roads had increased fourfold since 1970. It would never be less, only more. Forty million and forecast at exceeding a hundred million by the end of the century. vi) Environmentalist Donella Meadows' 1972 MIT thesis on world resources versus growth had been a bestseller since it was published; not because the public was worried about the future, they just thought it was a sci-fi novel – a thriller! Over the ensuing years, it had been proved correct on nine out of ten of its projected scenarios, the most alarming being the forecast of "total societal collapse" by 2040. Even Lorna had noticed that novels in Waterstones which a few years previously would have been in the sci-fi section had now been transferred to the social realism section. And if this wasn't already too much to contend with, vii) there was the incontrovertible evidence that mankind was being poisoned by plastic waste, illustrated by deposits found not only in many world water courses but even at the

Arctic circle and at the bottom of the Mariana Trench, seven and a half miles beneath the surface of the ocean. Things were changing, the insurance system would change, the whole economy was under threat of forced change. If you thought long and hard about it, Lorna's problems were relatively small. But that didn't help the way she was feeling now.

Three days had passed since she'd arrived at Chas's. The police had made another visit, again unannounced, though this time it was only the female who appeared at the door. The man stayed in the car. She'd confirmed that Diane Vigianno had been called to stand in for a sick delegate at a conference in Montreal at short notice. Promotion beckoned, it would seem. The Golightly course had been paid for in advance and rather than apply for the refund – minus her deposit – Diane had generously offered it to one of her office-bound colleagues, Stacey Albarn. Yes, not transferring the ID was extremely remiss and she was "devastated at the news", felt responsible, even though it was an unfortunate series of coincidences. She was also sorry for the additional work it had caused the police and Golightly. The policewoman had reminded Lorna that in the case of an inquest, Diane could be called to attend to confirm facts.

The second piece of information the police brought came as a surprise to Lorna. The post-mortem revealed that Diane – Stacey – did *not* drown. The lungs did not contain water; the cause of death was a heart attack. The divers had located the body not on the floor of the reservoir but against the outer shell of the spillway shaft, just below the surface of the water. If Lorna saw movement, she had imagined it. Stacey was not pushed, nor did she slip on those damp edging stones. She had been dead when her body entered the water.

'You probably won't hear from us again.'

The policewoman's news should have brought a degree of calm to Lorna, but it hadn't. Calm had been overridden by turbulence. Had it actually been the real Diane at Golightly, had it even been the real Diane who'd died, Lorna would have been a little more sanguine. But it wasn't, it was Stacey – why the *hell* had she been there? It was a coincidence too much to bear. '*Go on, skin up, Stace!*'

16

Lorna has been at Chas's for six days now. She hasn't been out and why would she? Chas does everything. He's even been over to Matching Thorpe on public transport to retrieve Lorna's Golf. So instead of it standing hard on the edge of the pit, it's sitting on the hardstanding out front, but she doesn't feel like driving. Chas cleaned it as well. It was covered with a layer of ashen dust which Chas removed, partly "on site" – sufficient to drive it to Buckhurst without too many people pointing at it or finger-drawing on its rear end. The rest of the muck he hosed away before giving it what he refers to as "the treatment". A great believer in wax, is Chas; he would have made a good valet if he hadn't become a schoolteacher.

He packed the teaching in last year. 'Twenty-five years!' he'd said, but it wasn't really like that. Chas said it was "a long slog with a lot of luck". Had a childhood which he never talked about, said there was something bad in him that had to be removed. A childhood tumour, Lorna wondered, but when he said "it didn't have to be there forever", she decided not to mention it again. But he had no qualms about boasting how he got from being a janitor to a junior teaching assistant in five years without any academic qualifications. Said he owed it all to a combination of his own motivation for self-improvement and other people's laziness. 'It's surprising how you can help out when other staff go off sick. All you need is a flu epidemic and, hey presto, you can find yourself running the handicraft class!' A great one for getting "on yer bike", is Chas.

The newspaper has given him more column space – at least, more often. 'Don't forget I've still got a mortgage to pay off,' he's always saying. Ye-es, could be future tensions between the two of them. Lorna paid hers off years ago. Should she have kept on paying into her company pension with Jay Natal for another five years? She just got her calculator out and the answer was a no-brainer. Who knew where she'd be in five years' time – enjoy it now! She had stocks and shares, was drawing income from various investments, and she still had the pittance of the state pension to look forward to.

Chas is doing a weekly column rather than monthly. Evidently, his readership is up three hundred per cent over the last two years – both online and paper editions. Chas's editor, Meredith, really likes Chas – the two of them have got quite pally. Chas has taken it upon himself to do charity work for a number of charities. Meredith and his wife have a child with special needs who has unusual musical talent, and they've established this charity for children in similar circumstances – Bessie's Fund, it's called. Chas doesn't put money in – he hasn't got any – he's donating time. It's made Lorna think she should give more to charities – she's got the money. Of course, it's the environment which is the main reason why Chas's column has gained popularity. People are taking it more seriously even though they can't actually do anything to make a real difference. That's what Lorna thinks, anyway. Chas thinks people *can* make a difference; *he's an optimist is our Chas*, that's probably why Lorna was attracted to him in the first place.

Lorna has to admit that, in a way, she's hiding at Chas's. The press has been trying to get her to do interviews. People and sinkholes seem to be a bewitching subject, with plenty of opportunities for some really corny headlines; *Down the plughole* or *That sinking feeling*, or so-and-so *found herself on the edge of the abyss.* Chas is worried for her, she can tell. 'Don't let them make you into a tabloid celebrity, Lorna!' He's never called her "Lorn" like most of her workmates, who of course it's difficult to keep up with now she's retired. She hasn't looked at any of her social media pages since before Golightly and she's only dealing with urgent phone messages. Her life now consists of a new time standard: BG and AG, that's Before Golightly and After. To have catch-up conversations with anybody would involve too much explaining. You can edit out a disaster you had on a creative writing course, but you can't not tell someone that your whole life has fallen into a sinkhole.

Lorna feels like a hunted criminal – criminal because she's caused a public nuisance. *Those people in Matching Thorpe, it was awful!* She's caused a mess at Golightly, but that wouldn't have happened if that bastard hadn't picked on her at the introduction supper and the following morning made an improper – to put it mildly – suggestion to her.

She's sleeping badly, hasn't had a decent night's sleep since before she arrived at Golightly. The problem is she seems to have loads of energy. She's even up in the morning before Chas, brings him a cup of tea. It was always the other way round before and she gets just a teeny-weeny feeling that Chas doesn't like that. He wants to be first in the farmyard. He does have his routines.

Sometimes he's up before dawn; it depends on the seasons and on the habits of whatever bird he's pursuing. Chas likes to walk or use public transport when he can, but to get to his nature spots car is the general rule. Walthamstow Wetlands is his principal haunt. Then he drives over to Little Russia, parks the car in one of the more salubrious streets, if he can find one, and has a wander around. Tottenham lad was Chas, or so he says.

Little Russia because he reckons his grandfather came over in 1917 to escape the revolution. Perhaps that's why he's an optimist? It's also perhaps why he's such a good mimic and can do a very authentic-sounding scouse? He can also be a bit of a bore and that is almost certainly the reason why Sheila left him, went off and got pregnant by somebody else before Chas could. Chas is the early bird who gets the worm, but only if it involves the first sighting of the willow warbler. When it comes to human relationships, Chas is a bit slow.

Let it not be said that Lorna doesn't love Chas, but something has happened over the last six days to their state of physical contact. Since early on in their relationship they've had separate bedrooms, but that's nothing to do with lack of physical intimacy, more to do with a twenty-first century condition of luxury when it comes to living space. That, and each being on their own for so long that sleep doesn't come easily without having a door between them. Lorna had been on her own in the house – the house that sank, that is – since Matt went off to Aus and married Rachel ten years ago. Even when Matt was a child, he was only with Lorna for short holiday periods. In those days – just as in these – eighteen was young to have a child, particularly when you'd decided not to tell the world who the father was, and she couldn't pretend that she wasn't grateful for Mum and Dad stepping in and bringing him up. Had it not been for Doug and Betty, Lorna would not be in the position of comparative good fortune which she is in now. The thing is, though, Lorna has to admit to herself that between Matt's dad – which wasn't a real relationship because hardly anybody knew about it anyway – and Chas, Lorna hasn't really formed any close relationships.

*

'You've been doing it again!' Chas is lying in bed, sipping the tea Lorna has brought him, looking uncomfortable that he's not up and she is. Lorna can tell that Chas is quietly amused about her little nocturnal habits of moving furniture around. It was, after all, only the pine Quaker settle in the hallway. It wasn't quite symmetrical. They've talked about it, it's not full-on obsessive compulsive disorder, more just a bit of rationalising things. It's happened before; he admits it wasn't quite in the right place, and she's not in denial of it or anything. If she was, then that would be a problem, they both agree, so fine.

'It's the stress of last week.' She says it as a joke, but they both know it's true. She's given Chas a pretty full account of what happened at Golightly; the weird first supper, the bossy introductions, the séance, but she's omitted to mention about receiving the message. She's concentrated on the positive points about the tutoring, the conversations and the general bonhomie. She has not, *not*, said anything about Spreighmont either picking on her after the supper or accosting her in the long sculpture gallery and saying, 'Fancy a quick shag?' I should think not! What indeed would poor old

Chas make of all that? Oh, she's told him she thinks the Golightly administration are suspicious, and that she wasn't the only person who thought that – and not just Diane… Stacey, that is… there were others; Boone, Drew, Nisi – pretty much everybody, even Juliet.

But carrying out a few interior design tweaks to the position of a hall settle is a far cry from tugging a chest of drawers in front of a door to barricade yourself against a sociopath. She hasn't told Chas about that. Far too crazy, too much of a touch of hysteria – not that Chas thinks she's prone to that. And what *does* Chas think of *her*? She can only speculate.

It's difficult to say. He never pursued her, it was she him after a real event networking session organised by the *Springhurst Mercury*, Chas's paper before he moved to the *Waltham Courier*. Chas isn't daft, she can only assume that he thought she liked him because basically she thought he was harmless. Who cares about a partner being a bit boring? I mean, which characteristic do you want in your partner, someone who's incredibly interesting, but edgy and unpredictable, or someone who's a little bit boring, but steady, loyal and reliable? Another no-brainer, surely? But there's a little more to it than that. Lorna spotted that Chas possesses a unique independence and if there's one thing that Lorna can't abide, it's needy men.

'I'm going to make you breakfast…'

Generally, the rule between them has been, he cooks in his house, she cooks when at hers, but she could be here for months, so there's going to be some changes, some improvements.

'If you insist. I'll just get myself into the shower.'
'Breakfast in bed.'
'What!'

Lorna suspects that Chas has never had breakfast in bed. Thinks, he thinks she's treating him like an invalid – or a lord.

'Go on! You're doing everything.'

Chas does all the cleaning. It's his house so that makes sense – except that Lorna has noticed that Chas has a special attraction to cleaning and hygiene. He's always insisted on hard floors everywhere in the apartment: wood, rubber or vinyl. Only the areas where you rest your feet while you're relaxing qualify to receive the luxury of a rug. Chas is frequently to be seen mop in one hand, bucket in the other. He's even confessed to liking that sound – you know, that tuneless clang you get when you put the mop bucket down onto the floor and the metal handle falls against the edge of the bucket. Yeh! Chas actually likes it – says he finds it calming.

'What about you?'

'I've had some coffee. You just relax, I'm going to have a shower.'

You can rely on most things in Chas's apartment and one of these is the inside of his cupboards. There's the one where the combi lurks, making its periodic gentle *whuup* sounds when someone turns the hot tap on, and there's the one where the towels are kept. Chas has them stacked on softwood slatted shelves, bath sheets in neat rectangles folded into four, hand towels folded three times in soft white piles. They have to be white, and they must be Egyptian cotton. According to Chas it has the longest, finest fibres, they're the most absorbent, and also the most durable. You'd think he was running a hotel. Lorna's towels are a motley collection of colours, some so old they were bought by her mother and so worn that they have acquired the texture of hessian. She takes a bath sheet and a hand towel from the cupboard where they've already absorbed warmth from the hot pipe travelling from the neighbouring combi cupboard. She goes into the bathroom, switches on the shower thermostat, then holding the folded towels in both hands she presses them to her face, first one cheek, then the other, then her mouth and nose, breathing in their softness. If towels could speak, it would be in the still of a lullaby; '*You have lost your house and home, but your comfort is here within me. I am your centre, let this be your nest, your place of rebirth.*' Lorna stands holding the towel to her face for an interval she is unable to quantify, then she switches on the water, slips out of her pyjamas and into the shower.

'Just for once.' Chas seems to have accepted Lorna's suggestion to relax, which is all to the good, because there's something Lorna's not quite sure about Chas this morning. It's not that he's distant, it's more as if he's planning something. She needs to be on her guard, and exercising more control over him should do the trick. An immaculately grey-suited figure standing at the corner of the east wing – it's no more than a flash.

In the kitchen, Lorna really has to think hard. It's not that Chas's cupboards aren't well organised – they are – nor is it that she doesn't know where he keeps everything. It's just that it's a week since she's done anything. A face behind a rusty grille, first Diane… no, Stacey, then the other one… she hardly dares say it to herself… the child. That awful foetus-like form. That's why she was so determined to have Matt, not to "consider termination" like some folk had advised her. Mum was all for it, Dad reluctant, Lorna could tell, but he came round to Mum's way of thinking and never looked back.

The thing was, she'd never told Mum and Dad about what had happened three years before, so they never really knew why she was so determined not to let Matt go. *He'd* taken care of everything – the man, she couldn't bring herself to say his name, even to herself, even after all these years. He was so much older, twice her age – Christ! He'd arranged it, she'd gone along with it, agreed, done it, that was it. Everything had been taken out of her hands and she was glad to be out of the situation, she'd been underage, for God's sake. Thought she would get over it, but when it happened again, she knew she hadn't. This time she told Mum, waited, thought it was better that way. Never mentioned the previous event; Mum must have suspected, Mums do, particularly when you're only fifteen; the deceit, the stealth, the ingenuity Lorna had to employ!

Black pudding? Not the kind of food that she would have expected Chas to be eating, but here it is, sitting in the fridge. Sausage, smoked streaky bacon, eggs – brown. What do you have that lot with? Tinned tomatoes – here we are – tinned baked beans. You wouldn't expect a watcher of wildlife to be eating this but here goes! Sliced white bread, soaked in olive oil and fried. She takes the bottle of extra virgin down from the cupboard. Holds it in her hand, its neck between her fingers and palm. She feels it's coolness as if it were a wine bottle held in the open air, thrown to her one November night. *''Ere, Lorn, you try!'*

No mushrooms? Hard luck! There's a red light, a tiny red light against the dark. She can smell cigarettes? Then she sees it's the cooker thermostat. Nobody's smoking, she hasn't smoked for years, Chas never – so he's always insisted. What she can actually smell is the relatively benign niff of a fridge that needs a bit of a clean. She'll do that.

She's grilling the sausage, bacon, and black pudding. That will leave plenty of space in the frying pan for the eggs and fried bread – eggs first, done, then add more oil, bring up to heat and get the bread sizzling. She serves it onto a large white plate, puts it down onto the work surface, stands back. That's a lot of food for one person. She leans forward, picks up the plate, and tips it all into the pedal waste bin, washes the plate – only the plate. She watches the water running out of the tall, shiny swan neck into the sink, down the plughole, down the spillway shaft. She can smell damp clothes, paper, smashed wood, atomised plaster and crushed herbs. Start again.

She's about to start her second attempt when she's conscious of Chas behind her. He steps on the pedal bin, sees the discarded food.

'Are you alright, Lorna?'

That question again! He's not just planning something. It's more than that. There's been a substitution. The real Chas has been got at. *Just keep cool, Lorna, we know who the "substitute" is, just don't let him know that you've spotted it.*

'I'm so sorry. I'm just not myself!' Lorna turns, checks herself; can she really embrace this person? For the sake of staying undercover, yes, she has to! She puts each of the palms of her hands over each of his shoulder blades. It's a loving gesture, genuine, the fake Chas will never suspect, *but we know who it is*, and when her left hand moves round and grasps the hand-stitched lapel of his dressing gown and her right-hand closes round his left ear, she screams.

'You didn't have to kill her!'

'Okay, Lorna, it's alright. I've got you.'

But it's not alright, and when she agrees to sit down and talk some more about it, she's already decided she's going to make a dash for it, to get out.

'I'm okay, really. I know you're not happy staying in bed.'

They both laugh, the kind of laugh which is halfway between coaxing and kidding.

'I'll have another go with the breakfast. I'm alright, honestly. You just go shower, then we'll both sit at the table, and I'll tell you everything.' She means it. She's got the black pudding, sausage and bacon out again. 'I'm fine.'

This time, it's looking good. Chas is satisfied. He's accepted. The main point is that they're going to talk it through. That's fixed in his mind, she can see that, so he can go shower now. When she hears the shower go on, she gives it one minute, on goes the bleeper that's telling him it's up to heat. He's in, and that's when she makes a run for the front door.

Lorna lifts the safety chain, fumbles the thumb-turn, and tugs the door towards her, doesn't shut it behind her. No time. Slides across the hall, another thumb-turn, and she's in the porch, padding down the front steps onto gravel. Why do her feet hurt? She pulls at the front gate – it's metal, not like her lovely blue wood one. It's rusty, gritty, cold, wet. She sees a short-lived image of a face, rubs her hands together. Which way? It doesn't matter because in the end they all lead the same way. Her face is wet, pixie hair beginning to drip. Everything out here seems enormous; why are the trees so big? Why can't she see very well? The children on their way to school on the other side of the road seem like spectres. It's so quiet. Something awful must have happened to society, another virus, the "big one". Moving is good, and the air is so cold. It will get the blood pumping. She could even try running, so lifts her knee, then the other one. It feels good. Her light dressing gown billows out, her pyjama jacket ruckled. Cars pass, their engines so soft and no more than a gentle hum. One of them draws up to the kerb and its passenger door opens.

A man gets out. He walks round the back of the car. He has to run briefly to catch up with her. He's carrying something, it's a mackintosh, hers, that very light one she took to Golightly. He holds it round her, guides her arms, first one sleeve, then the other.

'Put these on, Lorna.'

He's holding a pair of brown slip-on shoes, hers. She pulls off her soaking socks and fumbles on the shoes. He takes her hand, though hers is so cold now she can barely feel his. He leads her to the open passenger door, and she gets in, shuts the door, sits back, waits for him to walk behind the car, open the driver's door, get in, shut, start engine.

Lorna can see the passenger's mirror is down, can see her face in it. *What a mess!* She can also see that another car – a white one – has drawn up behind.

'Put the seat belt on, Lorna – here, let me.'

But Lorna is watching the car behind. The driver, a man, gets out, walks in front of the white car, stands and looks. Lorna catches his eye in her mirror. She can see that he has seen her looking at him.

'Not on your life!'

Lorna grabs at her door handle and the door swings open. As she raises herself out of her seat, the man next to her takes hold of the cuff of her mackintosh with his left hand.

'No, Lorna, please!'

Lorna has her left leg out of the car and resting on the road surface. Her right arm is being held firm by the man next to her. Lorna shifts her weight so her head and left shoulder are outside the car. She turns her head to her left.

'Help!'

The man from the car behind comes forward.

'Help me, please!'

'Do you want a hand?'

The second man takes hold of Lorna's left hand.

'Get off, will you!' The first man is shouting. 'This is my partner, she's in distress.'

'Oh, sure!' The second man does not "get off", he keeps hold of Lorna's left hand. There's a brief tug of war, but the first man does not have hold of Lorna's body, only the cuff of her mackintosh and, without warning, Lorna slips out of the mackintosh, runs past the second man, who has also let go, and she carries on running in the same direction as before, leaving the empty mackintosh draped over the seat and hanging out of the car. She tuns her head to look. The second man is tapping his smartphone.

'I'm calling the police.'

'I've told you, she's my partner, she's upset.'

'Oh yeah? Bastards like you!'

The second man walks away, talking into his phone. Gets back into his car, sits, bangs door shut.

Lorna plods on. She's no longer running and miraculously her feet feel dry, but she's lost that nice coat. The fog is so thick she can no longer see the schoolchildren on the other side of the road, only hear their disembodied shrillness. There's a hissing sound – no, it's somebody whispering. It's that car again – not the white one, the one with the man who brought her the coat. He's stopped the car and he's leaning across so that his head is near the open passenger window.

'Lorna, please!'

Lorna has only just glanced at him, so she turns her head back, looks straight ahead, and walks faster.

'Lorna, that man has called the police. He thinks I'm trying to kidnap you. We need to get to the doctor's surgery – it's just over there. We have to get there now, before the police come, otherwise I'll be in trouble. Not just trouble, terrible trouble. Lorna, do you understand?'

Police? Lorna has had enough of the police. Doctor? She knows she's not well, and her coat is still on the front seat of the car.

'I have to see the doctor – or a nurse. It's urgent.' Lorna looks at the digital clock behind the pale wood desk. It says 8.01. 'It's Mr Peake.'

'Date of birth?' asks the woman behind the reception desk.

'06/11/72.'

There's one other person in the room, sitting on a chair. Lorna is now wearing a face mask. The man brought one for her and himself.

'Chas?' asks the receptionist.

'Yes.'

'Can you tell me what it's about?'

'I'm the patient here, but this is my partner.' He turns his head towards Lorna. 'She's had two enormous emotional shocks in the last few days and she's not well. It's very urgent.'

She is troubled by thick-coming fancies. The voice of the woman behind the desk is calm, the voice of the man is agitated.

'Lorna. We know Lorna.'

The man seems surprised.

'You can see Dr Palumbo, the duty doctor. Just take a seat, please.'

Lorna? Who is Lorna? Who are these people talking about?

*

It's not a breakdown. A breakdown is a breakdown, and one must not venture to make judgements about things which one does not know. This, Lorna tells herself, is something called a fall-down, and something she has become all too familiar with; plunging down a sinkhole, plummeting a spillway shaft and tumbling down a rabbit hole. She *will* do the mindfulness course which Doctor Palumbo has recommended her to go on – but not at Golightly! Yes, she and Chas actually laughed about that one. An ironic laugh, but also genuine, liberating, and the first emotional outburst of the healing process. Lorna has become Alice, one minute too small, the next second too large. She has found herself in a strange land draped in a cloth whose weave is familiar but contains threads which are unfamiliar. She will try to see if she knows all the things she used to know, but she will not make the same mistake as Alice who thought that everything *had* to make sense. Lorna will try to accept that not only do some things not make sense they're not even intended to. Chas and she will do it together.

LORNA, CHAS &
THE RETURN TO GOLIGHTLY

17

I've never seen Lorna like this before, but then I've never known her witness the death of a colleague and only the next day lose her house and home. As I sit in my brown swivel chair in my study at Springhurst Hill, I can hear Lorna buzzing about the place, talking – sometimes to me but mainly on her phone. Right now, she's talking to the insurance people – she tells me Jason's left the company and Tobin's taken over. He says that the money could be in her account by the end of this month… or it could take up to a year! I know I was keen to have Lorna staying with me at first, but I don't know if I could stand that. I've got an article to write, *Autumn in the Wetlands* – Walthamstow Wetlands. For the last three months, I've been sending them pieces I'd written in advance. I need fresh material now so I must start work, but Lorna's incessant buzzing isn't conducive to my work.

Lorna's somebody who thrives on stress; she works through a situation, hammers it until she thinks she's on top of it, then hammers it again, just to make sure – or is it really that she just can't stop? But problems never exist in isolation, and, without her realising it, her life is a conveyor belt of crises. She went on the mindfulness course, does exercises – body mapping, meditation and stretch. She's even having sessions with a hypnotherapist. She's been having these repeat dreams – guilt feelings, she thinks they are – about her retiring early. She says that the hypnotherapist has got the perfect way of stopping these dreams. Evidently it requires something called, 'Personality duelling – or dualling – get it?' she said. The person who's having the dreams needs to get two chairs and place them opposite one another. Then you play at being two people. Person 1 says, '*Why are you making me have these dreams?*' Then Person 2 (that's Person 1, of course, who has to get up from the first chair and sit in the second chair) thinks of a reply such as, '*Because I think that you should have stayed working for another ten years.*' Then Person 2 goes back to being Person 1 and replies, '*You shouldn't be trying to tell me what to do.*' It's all very clever; duelling can become quite animated. You can even tell each other to fuck off. "The Hype" – as Lorna calls him – says it's all about "externalising" emotion and coming to terms with one's subconscious. Lorna likes it because it makes you feel like you've got another persona; it's a form of self-reinvention.

It's good to see it evolve – her recovery, that is. Even though we've been "together" for ten years, I realise that I know so little about Lorna. Well, I'm learning fast now, and what I've discovered is that she's pessimistic and depressive. It's not just what's happened, she's always been like that. I've got *my* friends – at the paper, and the Wetlands Club, that's it really. Then there's the old days, oh Christ! Reuben. Reuben is not a friend – well, he was, sort of, when we were kids. I just ran into him. It was bound to happen sooner or later.

Bad things happened and my life changed. It had to. Reuben can keep a secret. People say, 'How's Lorna?' but there's no way I can even start to tell them because everything's changing day by day. I'm wondering, what are people thinking? But *she's* not thinking like that, she's completely shut down on personal friends, except then I realised that not only does she not have any real personal friends, she doesn't want any. The only people she deals with are insurance brokers, bank, financial advisors, doctors, lawyers, and energy providers, and it's all on the phone. She's been here three months now and not once has she been out to the supermarket with me; she won't come out to eat, go to the cinema or theatre. She only went out to go on the mindfulness course. I buy, I cook, she chooses things but when she does it it's all online.

She's got this book, *The Building of Golightly*; it's a tome and she had to pay a fortune for it through Amazon because it's been out of print for years. She's always pointing bits out to me such as *Lord G* – that's the Earl of Golightly, evidently – *laid the design of a building, the likes of which should impress a king*, or one bit I like which is *digging ye foundations of ye grtt pile*. It's consuming her, but then that's what Lorna does – she hammers away. I would have thought that she would want to put Golightly well and truly behind her, but maybe it's therapy?

Something is happening with Lorna's appetite. She eats well – too fast if anything – but it's sex. It used to work well. I like slow, and she used to, before the

Golightly incident; touching, tasting each other – the tang, the trickle, the tickle. You know! She says it's different for a woman, but for me it's like gradually being drawn towards the edge of a cliff. You can't do that on your own because the need to be in control is too much. That's the beauty of sharing, the danger, the feeling of losing control. We all need to do it sometimes. I was a late starter – for various reasons – never really explored it with Sheila, she just wanted to get pregnant, and I didn't think I was ready to be a father, so in that respect I let her down.

Pre-Golightly, Lorna and I would enjoy what seemed to be pure comfort, the luxury of slowing time, the power of almost stopping the clock altogether. Then the bang – or rather, the being blown or pulled towards the edge, and finally falling over the cliff. For the man, the stage leading up to it and the moment when the epicentre of sensitivity inexplicably shifts from the top of the shaft, where it meets the glans – or foreskin if you've got one – to the testicles. If you were explaining it to your local GP as an ache in the balls, it's mild, it would be no more than one or two on the scale of one to ten – nevertheless not the sort of condition that's tolerable for long, so there's only one way to go and that's over the cliff, and ideally the two of you locked together in some mythological-style suicide pact. Lorna's always on about "the point of no return". She says that, for her, it's like adding the final gram to a weighing scales that sends it plunging. At that point – even if someone told her the roof was falling in on her

– saving herself or her partner wouldn't be the priority. Such is the power of the act of procreation, even if you're well past the menopause and you're not actually procreating.

Some people like to up the ante with danger stakes; extreme practices, ligatures, pain, oranges stuffed into mouths. I once read that a small incision made in the scrotum, and the partner gently blowing through a drinking straw inserted into the wound until the sack had inflated to the size and tautness of a pig's bladder, would produce an "incredible" orgasm. Fantasy or real, I was burned as a child. I understood the frisson of danger years ago, so I want safe. What Lorna and I do/did is relatively mainstream.

Lorna likes it in the bottom. She says it's quite healthy and normal to do it and to want to do it. I once had to go to hospital. They put a tube up my jacksie, told me I'd got something called diverticula, and that my sphincter was shrinking. So, should I be in a position where I was receiving it in *my cul-de-sac* I'd be hobbling around with a permanent fissure, so I'm just *not* wild about anal.

Then there's "the threesome". Oh yes, Lorna's talked about it often enough, told me about the two lipsticked beauties at Golightly that she fancied, and other occasions. She's also suggested another man. In fact, as far as I can gather, you can hire them – with waxed torsos like the Chippendales, perhaps even complete with bow ties? I know I'm a bit boring, but I was burned, and I want *safe*!

Before Golightly, Lorna introduced me to vocalising. This is a form of erotic operatic duet, apparently also intended to encourage each other to fall over the cliff, and at the same time. It was something new to me. With Sheila, it had all been a bit like a silent movie. Lorna says that women are naturally better at vocalising than men because they have an inbuilt intuition to pant during childbirth. I suppose it all should sound like Willard White's base tones resonating against Kiri Te Kanawa's soprano, except Lorna has an intensely mischievous habit of likening it to Cliff Richard's crooning and Hank Marvin's guitar riffing on *Move It*. As soon as the picture of the eighteen-year-old Cliff and the fret and fairy footwork of Hank enter my mind, then the sex session is well and truly over, with me convulsing – not by falling over the cliff, but collapsing, still at its brink and in helpless mirth.

Yes, Lorna really can be a little impish at times. She once booked the two of us into a polite bed and breakfast, where I recall that we gave one another a highly turbulent rodding against a sonorously vibrating bed headboard, which moments later I discovered was located less than ten feet and no more than a 30mm hollow-core door away from where families were gathering to eat silent breakfasts of proletarian cereals and tinned fruit. But since Golightly, before *any* of the aforementioned can happen, Lorna shouts, 'I want you inside me, now!' Her voice almost a stentorian duplicate of my mother's, when as a child I would hear it come barking up the stairs: 'I want you down here at this table, *now*!' Yet, even when I eventually arrived at my mother's table, there was precious little on it to sustain anybody.

Lorna is rarely vulgar in speech or act, but since Golightly I'm astounded at her outspoken coarseness.

'Go on!' she screams. 'Tweak my twat, munch my minge, pump my pussy and bang my back door, will you!'

It would be funny, that's if it wasn't all rather alarming. Was I nineteen years old, such forcefully erotic commands would undoubtedly induce an instant rock-hard penile condition, but now I'm fifty, diagnosed with hypertension, taking ramipril – "ram" being the non-operative word in this case, I have cold hands, cold feet, and a penis which is lamentably underfunded in blood. My cock shrinks to the size of a pencil stub. The doctor has – *of course, you might say* – prescribed Viagra, but it doesn't work one hundred per cent, and then there's the issue of spontaneity. Lorna's always been high on the scale of forceful-to-impetuous but it's as if something has got into her, something I can't define.

And there's something else. When Lorna texted me from the reservoir at Golightly, she asked me to research Golightly, the man, and this character Spreighmont. She's never mentioned it since, and I have a sneaking suspicion that not only did she not expect me to come up with anything, she didn't really want to know in the first place. Well, I *have* come up with something, I don't like what I've found, and as I sit here in my brown swivel chair wondering when I'm going to get the impetus to begin work on *Autumn in the Wetlands*, I can't make up my mind as to *how much* to tell her – or to even tell her at all.

*

I'm looking at an email which landed in my inbox precisely five minutes ago.

> *Hello, Chas – Phil, I should say.*
>
> *Since we ran into one another I've been thinking. I wonder if you might do me a little favour. You see I've applied for this job – a teaching job – and I know you're a teacher now, and I need a reference. You'd be perfect, Phil, because you came up the hard way and your word will go a long way. I need this job very badly, because like you, Phil, my life needs to change.*
>
> *Your old mate, Reuben*

I just ran into him, that's all. It was weeks ago – while Lorna was at Golightly. A chance in a million, it was never meant to happen like that. How he recognised me? If it had been in Hero Road in the old days in "the Wool" that he'd seen me, understandable. But it was in Tottenham! He said it was the way I walk… *They shall know them by their gait*. He caught me totally off guard. 'Phil!' he said, and I only said, 'Yes?' But there was no denying it then. Then he said, 'It's a long time since we was in Jerk-in-Bed.' I said I was in a hurry and I naively thought that was that. What amazes me is how he got my email address, but then why should it? It's easy, you just need time and Reuben's got plenty of that. He must have followed me and he probably knows everything about me. Except the paper, apparently, he thinks I'm still teaching. The teacher job is a load of crap, of course, he's blaggin' me 'ead. I know I struck lucky and got there in stages, but Reuben wouldn't even get to first base. He wants money, but he'll never say that because that would be blackmail. Well, he's not going to get it. It's clever, because I can't go to the police – well, not about that anyway.

I will not have that gobshite Reuben fuck up the rest of my life.

18

Springhurst Hill, Essex: Distance from London – ten miles. Tube station – Springhurst Hill, Central line. Travel time between Springhurst Hill and Oxford Circus – thirty-five minutes. This was great when I was working at Jay Natal's. Equally good if I was commuting from Matching Thorpe. I would park and ride – drive to Epping at the end of the Central line, sixteen minutes, then sit there for forty-five minutes, get off at Oxford Circus and walk down to Hanover Square. Before JNs moved there, they were in Wigmore Street, so I just got off at Bond Street. Happy days! If I was staying over at Chas's, I'd drive to Springhurst, then commute the thirty-five-minute tube journey in the morning, a doddle! Being here endlessly now seems odd.

It's a peculiar place – Springhurst. Suits Chas to a tee, says it feels like a seaside town without the sea. '*I miss the sea, you know!*' Come on, Chas! Tottenham? When you come out of the tube station, the land opposite you slopes gently and Chas's apartment is two short streets uphill. You stand, look over the roof of the tube station and your eye just keeps on going. There're no tall buildings, no landmarks, just scrappy roofs of bungalows, then fields, there's no hills. *Springhurst Hill; elevation above sea level 130 feet* – so no real hills. Chas doesn't like hills. Whenever we've been on holiday together, we've gone to places like Rye, Orford Ness and Blakeney. Chas has never been abroad – must be a record. Says he's never wanted to. He's never even bothered to get himself a passport.

Queens Road is the main social street in Springhurst – it's where all the bistros, bars and restaurants are. Even most of those buildings are only one storey, taller ones generally at a corner. I think it looks like a wild west town, saloon bars on every corner, as if there could be frequent shoot-outs. There have been muggings, but nothing worse. Practically everybody here is dependent on London.

'Why don't we go to The Son of Man?'

Chas looks surprised. 'Half of the Essex aristocracy will be there. It's posh twat, not meant for local people!'

'Cha-as!'

Chas refuses to call them Springhur*sters*, he thinks it's far too "peoplespeak". The Son of Man – perhaps somewhat incongruously – is the local church which has recently reopened after a major makeover into a restaurant. With its spire, it's the tallest building in the town.

'If you insist, it's *your* birthday.' Chas is secretly pleased, I can tell. He's wanted to go in there the minute he found out they were converting it into a foodery and, yes, it's my fifty-sixth birthday.

The rule between us has always been that when he's in Matching I pay for any eating out, and when I'm in Springhurst, he pays – except now is different because I'm here indefinitely so I'm paying fifty per cent of all food bills. There is another way of looking at it, in that my Jay Natal pension – even though I cashed it in five years early – amounts to over five times what Chas is earning at the *Waltham Courier*, so unless Chas gets headhunted by the *Financial Times*, we're never going to be financial peers. For the purposes of this evening, we've agreed to go halves. That's because The Son of Man isn't £s or ££s or £££s, or even ££££s. It's categorised on Strip Advisor (yes, Strip I like to call it) as "blow out", aimed at turbo-charged aspiring Essex folk. It *is* a deconsecrated church, for God's sake!

When you Google it, as well as the "*about us*", "*home*" and "*menus*", there's an FAQs section with cringe-making bullet points: "*No, we don't supply communion wafers, all our wafers are gluten free made with organically grown west country maize*", or "*Our wines come from all over the world including South Africa, New Zealand and France; they never run out, so there's no need for anyone to turn water into wine here"*, or *"The management do everything possible to ensure that you enjoy your meal here, and we sincerely hope it will not be the last supper you have here"*.

'I'm surprised they've left all the gravestones vertical. If they'd laid them down flat, they'd make perfect hardstanding for all the McLarens, Lotuses and SUVs that get parked on the road outside.' Chas can be droll.

'We could walk there?'

'Of course!' Chas certainly won't be indulging in that antisocial habit of parking with one wheel in the road and the other in the middle of the pavement.

It's a lovely evening. Warm, seven o'clock, long shadows, and quite clearly Monday isn't their busiest night; the road by the church is almost empty. There's a lychgate, would you believe? Pointy roof and round arch made from black wood, and next to the gate, where the list of religious services would normally be posted, is the sign, *The Son of Man*, hanging from a gallows type wood frame, and what it shows is immediately familiar to me. It's from a painting by a Belgian artist, whose name escapes me, but it's the figure of a man wearing a dark overcoat, white shirt, red tie and standing in front of a low stone wall. Behind the man is sea and sky, though it's not possible to tell where each meets the other. The figure is posing formally, hands by his sides, and on his head is a bowler hat. You can see the shape of his face, his ears, and his chin, but not his features because suspended in front of his head is a large green apple dangling from a branch which has several leaves. It's almost as if the man is a tree whose sole purpose is to bear fruit. Somewhere he has an identity, but he's lost it, and if the air around me wasn't so warm I would shudder. I glance at Chas, he doesn't like it either, I can tell.

Standing behind a large glass door which opens automatically and noiselessly, I can see that the maître d' is dressed exactly as the man in the painting except a suit instead of overcoat, no bowler hat, and, perhaps surprisingly, his smile isn't just welcoming, it's mischievous, as if he's amazed to find himself working here, and yes, it is all a bit strange and possibly rather pretentious, isn't it? I'm taken aback – nay, overwhelmed by how bright it is in here; chandeliers, great foaming gobbets of light, but they don't hurt. It's like looking at a thousand candles. Chas is opening his mouth to say, '*Peake, seven o'clock, the quiet table for two,*' but the dapper maître knows that. We've no coats to take, so he hands us over to a female who is dressed exactly as the man, but scarf instead of tie, and three-quarter length skirt. There's a look of the 1940s about her and for one moment I think it's Elaine Wayfarer or Rita Ellcock come from Golightly to haunt me, but it's not and her smile, like the maître d's, is genuine – I'm sure of it.

She escorts us to our table and it's beautiful. Everything seems to be in booths; soft, dark banquette seating, and a pale disc apparently floating above our heads when we're seated. It looks as if it's made from velvet, but it can't be because there are three candles burning merrily in the centre of the table. When we sit down it's like you're in a world of your own, you're just conscious of the occasional suited figures drifting past. There's a vague scent of vanilla.

'Why didn't we dress up more?'

'You look perfect as you are.' Chas can be so diplomatic.

'I thought it would be all pine and beams.'

'There *are* beams, on the ceiling.'

I know what he *means*, but sitting where we are it doesn't feel church-like at all, it's more moon station. I'm tapping the tabletop.

'Look at this table, it's like marble but it's warm.'

Another Elaine Wayfarer-type girl appears with the champagne. If I was thinking cynically, and in another context, all this smiling could get you down, but it's sincere, it's as if the whole place exudes happiness. I can hear organ music, neither intrusive nor sinister. Perhaps it's Bach, but I don't recognise it. There's no menu; when you book you just tell them what your dietary requirements are and put your trust in the chef, who is evidently Michelin zillions of stars.

'Cheers, Lorna. You're so much better, in fact, I'd say you're smashing it.'

'What do you think?' Trying to get Chas to open up isn't easy. 'I mean, I didn't expect this.'

'Neither did I. Essex man thrives on clichés, has a need for the predictable, he likes to feel in control. This is on the edge of being out of control, and probably good for us all, occasionally.'

'It's so quiet; where is everybody? How do they make a profit? All this must have cost a fortune.'

The girl reappears and sets up the table. She's followed closely by a second girl with the starters. They come with a printed card with a copperplate-style font, rather like an olde worlde business card. It tells you what you're eating. Chas has been given *Aged Beef Tartare* – Chas, beef? Everybody assumes Chas is a veggie because he's an environmentalist, but *tartare*? He's just going to go through with it for the hell of it. He's been in that kind of mood for a while, I can tell. The beef tartare comes with: *alliums, turnip, oscetra caviar*. Mine is *Mushroom Tartlet, slow-cooked egg yolk and puffed barley*.

'Where are we going, Chas?'

He's ready for the question. '*You* are going to find yourself the most fabulous house, but it won't be like Matching Thorpe.'

'I know that. I meant where are *we* going?'

'I think we're good.'

'Smashing it?'

'You could say.'

We are an odd couple. I know it's not unique for two only children to get together, sometimes they seem to be magnets to one another, and having no siblings can be a mixed blessing. On the one hand there's no rivalry, no one to compete with for the love of the parents, and when the old dears get really old and in need of care, there's no interfering voice at the other end of the telephone telling you that you need to do this or that. On the other hand, the buck stops with you, and like it or not there's never another family member to confer with. I think my parents died when they did because they were worn out from bringing up Matt. Of course, they didn't expect their daughter to be having a baby with an unidentified father, in her first year at college. They never regretted it, but they should have been enjoying their middle years and old age. I've felt guilty about that. As for Chas, he never talks about his parents, and I just have to accept that. I don't probe.

'What I mean is, here's me enjoying living what amounts to a – hopefully creative – retirement, while you're still slogging away paying off your mortgage.' I've even offered to pay it off for him and he won't accept. He's right, of course; not just pride, it's independence.

'It's not slogging, Lorna, and it is creative. All I'm doing is like what a lot of people call a hobby. Most think of work and leisure as two separate things; this is both rolled into one and I couldn't have wanted for better.'

Chas didn't get the mortgage easily: he could only manage the deposit and interest-only payments when the full-time handicraft teaching money started coming in, and he could only cope with full repayments when he got the newspaper work as well. Before that he was renting through a housing association; owning property for him was a dream.

By now my eyes have adjusted to the unfamiliar ambience and I can see out and into the penumbra outside our little seating coral. There are paintings on the walls of the church; I was vaguely aware of them as we were steered under pointed arches and between chubby stone columns. I'd assumed they were stations of the cross. But they're small, framed reproductions of popular famous paintings. Beyond Chas's left ear I can see the gaunt and shaded face of Arnolfini and if I tilt my face slightly to my left, it gives the impression that Arnolfini's sombre-hued broad-brimmed hat is sitting on Chas's head. I'm smiling.

'What?'

'I'm not laughing at what you said; it's just that there are paintings on the walls and it looks like you've got Arnolfini's floppy hat on your head.'

For a moment Chas looks worried, twists himself round while he scans the walls.

'Essex man art.'

'Now then, Chas, don't scoff!' I'm feeling playful. 'Just 'cos you like Jeff Koons.'

Chas snorts. 'I *don't!*' His voice rises an indignant octave.

'I'm only joking, love.'

Let it not be said that Chas is ignorant of culture, anything but. But instead of doing what most people who came up the hard way – didn't go to college and that, or maybe didn't even finish school, for all I know – do and become experts at quizzes and crossword puzzles, Chas reads the *Guardian*, *Telegraph*, *Times* arts pages. He can, should the fancy take him, not only talk long and loud about the films of David Lean, he can also tell you about the films of David Lynch, and he's become a well-informed – and apparently well-followed – environmentalist.

'There's *The Scream*, and I can just see *The Persistence of Memory* behind the maître d's desk.'

'Is everything alright?' It's the "Son of Man" himself come to check if we like the food.

'Lovely, thanks!'

'Each person needs to develop in their own way at their own pace. People are always on about "achievement" – high achievers, and being aspirational—'

'Society's very materialistic—'

'No, I don't mean that. I'm not jumping on the anti-materialistic bandwagon. I would just argue that not everybody is in the position to make achievements. But *everybody* can develop.'

'What's the difference?'

'As I say, not everybody is in a position to achieve, but anyone can develop. We all have a starting point, and what really counts is, have you moved on from what you were yesterday? What I'm criticising is the situation like an artist who produces technically "brilliant" pictures that win prizes and sell like hot cakes, but years down the line, has he changed? Has he developed? Same with novels – anything. No point in having all those prizes and all that money if you're still producing the same formulaic stuff, so I suppose the argument is more about becoming a victim of commercialism rather than materialism. Everybody can develop, even people with disadvantages – particularly people with disadvantages. Some people can naturally keep reinventing themselves, others have to learn it, in fact, it's probably the only thing one can really learn, the capacity to be able to change. I'd ban the word "achieve" from my lexicon and replace it with "development".'

The organ music has been replaced with Baroque and definitely Bach this time, the *Cantatas*, the one with that lovely trumpet – the one that McCartney used in *Penny Lane*. Trouble is, Baroque reminds me of Golightly. The mains arrive; Chas has been presented with *East Coast Cod, celeriac, maitake, dashi vinegar, whey sauce and coastal herbs*. I'm about to tuck in to the veggie option: *Jerusalem artichoke, truffle and hazelnut pesto, buckwheat gnocchi and braised leeks.*

'Do you really think that people can change that much, Chas?'

'From what?'

'Well, what you are – were.'

'It depends what your starting point is. I was interested in the way you were saying that the subject of spies and spying had come up when you were on the course at Golightly. Now there's a breed of people who undergo change, and they do it – for professional reasons, of course – because they've been given new identities. Nobody can *really* change unless they disappear and then turn up with a new identity – people who have faked their own death: John Stonehouse, Aleister Crowley.'

'Stonehouse got found out, and Crowley, well, that's a truly weird one.'

'I know, I'm just using the idea to illustrate what I mean. People around them don't know them so can't make assumptions about them then, can't carry on sticking the same label on them. Makeovers are all very well, Lorna, but they're worthless if the person underneath doesn't develop – or the product, for that matter.'

Chas isn't deliberately trying to be hurtful about marketing, he's just being truthful. He has this awful quality of being able to see through things, like some shaman. It's good for me.

'You see, Lorna...' There's a look in Chas's eye I haven't seen before, almost a countenance of evangelical fervour. 'I don't wish to repeat myself, but people don't understand the difference between achievement and development, and when that Last Judgement comes...' – I see his eye roving the walls of the church, perhaps half-expecting (and probably fearful) of seeing Michelangelo's titanic work for the Sistine Chapel in the form of some pygmyised cheap reproduction – 'and they get to the gates of heaven, and they're asked, "What have *you* done with your life?" and they answer, "I've achieved X and Y," they'll be told, "So what? What we want to know is have you developed? Right then," the people at the gates of heaven will say, "well in that case you can just fuck off down to hell!".'

'Cha-as!' Chas hardly ever swears.

'Why? Because they failed to develop, they've wasted their lives. It's what we're here for, Lorna, to search for and discover our own unique creativity. Not just to achieve coupledom, and to have families. Not to produce children which the earth is finding increasingly impossible to feed, not to become just another consumer while telling ourselves we're being creative. Not to let ourselves be hoodwinked into believing that what marketeers call "choice" is being inventive. Not to compare ourselves to the next person, but to quietly get on and do something with our lives by simply being better than *we* were yesterday…'

I can see the Son of Man hovering. He's going to ask us, "Is everything alright?", but he can see that Chas is mid-rant about something, so he withdraws.

'We delude ourselves, we kid – not just each other but ourselves. We feel pumped-up – loved, even – because we have seven thousand followers on Twitter, Instagram, or "friends" on Facebook. But how many of those are genuinely interested in us, or we in them? How many are real, flesh and blood, huggable, smellable, kissable people? We can't all be pop stars, or media personalities flippantly sharing their neuroses with a gullible mass audience, causing media hysteria. What about the ordinary man or woman – and it's increasingly the man – young or old who, through a supreme strength of will, has checked into a doctor's surgery and asks at reception, "I'm worried about my state of mental health and welfare, can I please see a nurse straight away?" If we can do that and actually get help, then that's real progress in society. I know, because I hit bedrock and there was nothing like that for me…'

Something amazing has happened. Chas has actually opened up, so I'm just sitting here and letting it all pour over me. In fact, it feels like cod liver oil, almost soothing, that is, until the point just after you've swallowed it.

'We con ourselves, Lorna, over the environment – believe me, I've been researching it for over ten years. It's not that we're ignorant, the pointers have been there for us from all angles for decades, be it E.F. Schumacher or B.F. Skinner – except that ninety-nine per cent of the population thinks that Schumacher is a motor racing driver, not a statistician and economist, and that Skinner is a stand-up comic, not a behavioural psychologist. We've chosen to put on blinkers, but we've had no choice because it's that old figure of speech the runaway train. When the breaks fail on a downward slope it just gets faster and faster, and that's the world, Lorna, overladen, overpopulated and over fuelled.

'"Mother Earth's a tough old bird, she'll come round", is what they say – the environmental doubters, the global-warming blinker-wearers. Well, they would say that, wouldn't they? Just like any serial wife-beater or psychological abuser.

'Imagine, Lorna, homo sapiens has been around for almost three hundred thousand years yet global warming only began three hundred years ago at Coalbrookdale in Shropshire when it was discovered that you could smelt iron from coke instead of the iron age-old method of burning charcoal and wood. Visualise that as a pie chart-style clock, Lorna, three hundred years seen on the face of a three-hundred-thousand-year clock? That's 0.012 seconds to midnight, yet it's taken us just that long to bugger up the world – and there's worse. Switched-on historian environmentalists like Peter Frankopan reckon that the majority of damage which has accelerated global warming has happened since he sat his A-levels! The man's barely fifty, our age…'[ii]

Oh Jesus! I suddenly have a heart-freezing thought. In a fit of penitent curiosity, I'd once calculated that when my unborn baby was killed, its heart had beaten just two million, eight hundred thousand times – had anybody bothered to detect it at ten weeks gestation, that is. That was, in relation to the two-and-a-half billion times its heart should have beaten had it lived till the age of eighty, in other words, just 0.012 of what it should have done had that small organ gone on thumping away in that body without a break until the point of natural death. The calculation was chillingly similar.

'Everything's happening so fast, the train is out of control, people can't adjust – yes, like the poor wacker in the doctor's surgery. And while that wacker is sitting waiting to be called to see the nurse, his mind may be fucked, but his thumb is still operating perfectly because out comes his smartphone and he's on social media. We're running, Lorna, we're hiding. As a civilisation our real time social skills have sunk so low that we now actually believe that what we're doing on a smartphone is having a proper relationship.

'So, of course everybody's donned blinkers. That's why when conversations in a pub or dinner party turn to the environment, some wag invariably shouts in a John Laurie-style voice, "We're all dooooomed." And guess what? The discussion closes down because there's nowhere for it to go after that.'

'Rather like saying, "I blame the Tories".' I'm thinking of Jenna's comment on that fateful evening at Golightly.

'Then there's the less switched-on historians who croak away saying, "We've been through ice ages before, we've survived the Black Death". But it's not comparable! We have *not* been here before; we're in unchartered territory. Except what we do know is that it's either a flood or a virus which will eventually get us. These are simple truths, Lorna, *truths*, not necessarily facts, and if an uneducated tosser like me can grasp that, then why not the millions of *Guardian*-reading PhDs?'

'Because they're worrying about their shares in fossil fuels, and also it's just intractable, Chas, so they reach for their blinkers and hope to God that our grandchildren can invent something to keep life going.'

'And there's something else. Robert Oppenheimer's famous comment made after the first atomic bomb test in New Mexico in 1945, "Now I am become death, the destroyer of worlds," has come to have a new meaning insofar as Oppenheimer was both right and wrong. Wrong to believe that the world would end in nuclear holocaust – sure, there's always the danger of the fool, the rogue state or the unstoppable system, but for the last eighty years the hydrogen bomb has served humanity as a deterrent against nuclear war. It's one of the few deterrents that has worked – capital punishment certainly didn't. But Oppenheimer was right in that it's technology with all its pollution which is destroying the world. It's just happening slowly through global warming instead of in a series of escalating big bangs.

'When the Space Race ended with the moon landings in 1969, there was a real opportunity to slow down, to rethink and reinvent. It wasn't too late to stop global warming then, and the philosophy was there to support it. It's apt that Oppenheimer referred to the Hindu verse scripture of the *Bhagavad Gita*, which is a lesson on desire, wealth and righteousness. But nothing slowed down, Lorna, it just got faster, using technology to produce more of the same, to serve; pride, greed, wrath, envy, lust, gluttony and sloth. No matter how much you sneer at hippiedom with its basic tenets of love and peace, it's not difficult to see how mankind has made a terrible mistake. The human experiment peaked in the late 1960s, but it's failed now, Lorna. Mankind has slipped into irreversible decline. I'm so sorry not to be more positive.'

I'm aghast. Chas's shoulders are shaking, his face is wet, his eyes suddenly swollen and for a split second I recall the chilling moment at the reservoir when I believed that Stacey was weeping by the lake. Never once since I met him have I doubted Chas's sincerity. I could so easily have taken his hand and squeezed it. But instead of extending empathic fingers, I find myself distancing myself from his emotion, as if I really believe that he's play-acting. I'm ashamed, but I'm defensive so I'm humouring him. All I can think of is that the beef tartare, the champagne and a glimpse of Dali's *The Persistence of Memory* have coalesced into a potion which has turned Chas into a raving William Blake, experiencing one of his mystical visions on The Rye at Peckham.

'Sorry.'

I'm sorry for covertly humouring him now, but I'm still guarded. I can see that I should be ashamed, but I can't help it.

The Son of Man drifts into view. 'Is everything alright?'

'Yes, lovely, thanks.' I'm glad he doesn't stay and talk.

I can see more people in the restaurant now, mainly couples but there's the occasional party. They're all about our age… well, they would be with the price tag! Some of them have dressed up a bit – mainly the women. I'm wearing Chas's birthday present to me, an antique glass pendant in silver mounting. I love it; I know it's inexpensive, but the value is in its unusualness and appropriateness, not market value. It tells me that Chas knows me, knows more about me than probably I know about myself – or than I've been prepared to admit to myself! Certainly, more than I know about him. It's also a great sign that people no longer need to travel to some distant region of the world to buy something exclusive. They can get it on eBay.

The desserts arrive, so we swap cards and Chas has been given *Essex rhubarb, spiced pain perdu, almond, mascarpone, yoghurt and blood orange.* I've got *prune and brandy soufflé, melted ice cream, burnt citrus and salted caramel.*

We skip coffee; I deal with the bill while Chas goes off to the gents. We like to get our priorities right. I watch him springing up the white-painted staircase leading to the giant mezzanine they've put in. I'm okay, even after half a bottle of champagne.

'What's it like upstairs?'

'It's divided into private dining rooms. One window each – divided, of course, by the floor, but it looks good.'

'What about the toilets?'

'Didn't notice, except outside the ladies' they've got *The Garden of Earthly Delights.*'

'What about the gents'?'

'*Whistler's Mother.*'

As we're saying cheerio to the staff, I notice that the painting in the glass entrance lobby is *The Night Watch.*

We're just walking under the lychgate when Chas tells me he's left his phone in the Gents.

'I'll hang on here; it's a beautiful night.' It's dark now.

When it's quiet, and you're on your own standing in a state of what might be called dead time – and outside a church, you can't help it, your mind becomes vulnerable to ear worms. *There was I, waiting at the —, waaayting at the—* shut up! Hate it, dreadful cockney rant. It was a favourite of my dad's. He would sing it when Mum was washing up in the kitchen and when he got to the bit about not being able to get away to the church to marry the girl in the song because he's married already and his wife won't let him, a hateful look of resentment would come over his face. Mum would pick up a serving spoon and bang loudly on the kitchen work surface to drown him out.

I'm so busy being irritated by my earworm that I haven't heard the *pap-pap* and clatter of a motor scooter. The driver is a boy of about sixteen, the passenger quite a bit younger. In fact, I'm so preoccupied with how young they look that I leave myself no time to prepare, as the smaller boy slides off the back and lunges at me. I feel a sharp tug at my neck and there's a snipping sound, a softer tearing sound and I'm conscious that my shoulder bag has gone. There's something missing from round my neck as well. The smaller boy runs round the corner and into an alleyway while there's a renewed burst of clattering from the scooter engine as it moves a few feet towards where the boy is. I'm petrified, then I blunder after the younger boy who I can see is standing, torch in hand going through my bag. He drops the bag, dashes out of the alley towards his mate, and straight into two large dark figures who grab him. The motor scooter clatters off into the night.

'Got you, you little bastard!' The two men are maybe early forties. One has the boy up against a brick wall, the other man is poking his smartphone.

'We've been trying to get these for months.' He's talking to me, but I'm too shocked to reply. The more overweight of the two men has his face close to the boy.

'You, my lad, are in trouble…' The man thrusts his face closer to the boy's, their noses are touching. 'For what you are about to receive is going to be the biggest fucking hiding of your little fucking waste of a life.' His huge hands have the boy by the neck, the boy's head is wobbling, his feet have left the ground. 'You, my worthless little shit, are about to experience what is known as a *genuine* Essex kicking.'

There's another voice. 'On top te fuck!' And then, 'Leave him alone, he's only a kid.' It's Chas, just come up behind me. 'I'm *so* sorry Lorna, I shouldn't have left you.'

'The police are on their way.' The other man has backed off.

'If you touch him, you'll regret it. Leave it to the police.'

'They do fuck all.'

A police car arrives, and another one. Then a van. Two policemen and two policewomen. The van crew stay in their seats.

'These guys have been doing all this area; Chigwell, Woodford, Loughton.' The more aggressive man has released his grip and the policewomen take over.

'Are you hurt, madam?'

Another male dressed like The Son of Man has appeared.

'Come and sit down inside.' We walk back towards the restaurant door, leaving the police and the boy. It's very good of the restauranteur; they didn't need to come out and investigate.

'Are you sure? This isn't good for your business.'

'You'll be better for sitting somewhere comfortably. The police can follow to take any details they need. Our guests,' he calls them, not customers, 'won't notice the odd policewoman calling at the maître d's desk. Would *you* have done?'

'No.' He's right.

Chas and I are seated back in the restaurant, just inside the glass door. I feel no sympathy with the boy, not that I would have behaved like the two vigilantes, but I'm angry. My bank cards and jewellery will no doubt be returned to me, but it's an assault, another assault. Chas has shown extraordinary restraint, and I don't quite know what to make of that.

'Can we get you anything while you wait?'

'No, but I'll tell you what, I'd like to use your garden of earthly delights.'

Amazingly, he knows exactly what I mean.

19

'Chas, look at this! "*A settlement, dwellinges consisting of fifty small houses and local farmhouses, each with its own strip of land.*" It all had to be demolished, then flooded to create the lake. Somewhere at the bottom of that lake are the foundations of those houses. It wasn't as if they were building on virgin land, hundreds of people had to be moved.'

'Maybe they rehoused them?'

'It doesn't look as if they did. Evidently, it was called "emparkment", like "empowerment"; the ruling classes were empowering themselves by means of emparkment.'

'It happened a lot *then*; evictions, "clearances". It happens now – particularly if they're tenants. People get notified that a Lidl or Aldi store is going to be built on where they're living and telling them they must leave.'

'It says: "*Innumerable people involved in the supplye of lead, nailles, brickkes, and the removing of earthe.*" Look at the old spelling!'

'Perhaps the inhabitants were employed on the building work?'

'They were farmers, Chas. Some of them would have building skills but it seems that many of the building workers were brought in from elsewhere. Golightly wasn't the only one building round there, that part of the country had become a mecca for master craftsmen – some from Europe, look at the names! Project manager – Dijkman, architect – Cornelissen, surveyor – Meulenbelt, mason – Bouwman. Berkenbosch, Bijl and Timmerman – all to do with woodworks.'

'Meulenbelt – surveyor, but they've got an English surveyor as well, Ainsworth, but there's a note against his name saying "*illiterate*", so maybe that's why there's the two of them working together?'

'Or was he a trainee?'

Chas thinks I'm mad. He thinks I should leave the whole thing behind. Forget about Golightly, choose another creative writing course somewhere else, and start again. But I know I'm right. Getting to know more is the only way I can get it out of my system. There's that crazy message for me via that so-called medium. I haven't forgotten; it's safe. I decoded it, well, substituted the numbers for letters, but it doesn't make any damn sense. Latin? French? It doesn't even look like a foreign language. I shan't throw it away, but I really don't think that it was anything more than something that grew out of the excitement of that first evening.

Chas has forgotten something: I asked him to find out about Golightly… and that vicious little cat Spreighmont, and in a way I'm quite glad he's forgotten. If I want to know something, it's me that's got to dig for it. It's only us that can reinvent ourselves, others can't do it for us; I should know, I'm the marketing expert. But I know damn well he won't have found anything out. He'll have just been sitting there in his brown swivel chair worrying about his column – newspaper column, that is, but there *is* his other column, the one between his legs that hasn't been very column-like recently. Don't worry, Chas, I know he's only fifty, but some men just don't produce as much testosterone as they did when they were thrusting teenagers. I don't mind, I don't think about sex for weeks sometimes. Chas does his best.

'Chas, I've found out that Golightly was a bit of a bad boy. Not the Nosferatu character that's there now, I mean the third earl. Evidently, he was connected to the 1745 rebellion to oust King George II and it says here "*attainted*", which I gather means he had all his estate confiscated. He was lucky to escape with his life.'

'That's why there's no mention of the name Golightly until recently. The Earl of Parksfield and Golightly aren't the same; not only that, Parksfield the man never existed. After 1746, the estate went to the Crown and passed to the government during the nineteenth century. The saying "The title was the land, and the land was the title" was no longer the case. Only ten years ago, there was a thing in the news saying that they'd found old documents proving that Golightly wasn't as involved in the rebellion as first thought, and the name was reinstated. That's when Nosferatu, as you call him, seemed to appear on the scene. Interesting that the house was government-owned and that *our* Golightly is ex-MI5.'

'How do you know all this, Chas?'

'I've been digging. Surely *you* remember the publicity anyway?'

'I was completely wrapped up with Paco Rabanne at the time, I missed a lot of mainstream news items. Tell me what else was happening around the same time.'

'You were meeting *me*!'

Chas can be so funny, but right now I feel he's a little edgy.

'I've found out a few other things.'

'Really?'

He sounds hesitant, as if he doesn't want to tell me.

'Not about Golightly, he's a blank, but that wacker Spreighmont.'

'Oh, yes?' I'm making it sound offhand, as if he'll change his mind and say "Oh, nothing really", but he's quite agitated, I can tell.

'I went to the police.'

'*Did* you?' I'm sounding surprised, I just can't help it.

'You can get access to files from thirty years ago, and names – some of them anyway. If they've involved violence.'

'And…?'

'Well, unsurprisingly, Spreighmont isn't his real name. Nor is he a knight of the realm. His name is Nick Jones. And once you've got a name, it seems, there's something called "the right to ask".'

I'm wondering how I should react; interested, nonchalant, concerned, baffled? I think interested is best for now.

'He's got a criminal record from when he was a drama student. Relatively minor offence, possession of cannabis, but it escalated into violence. There was an incident, which weirdly enough occurred at Golightly, except – as we both now know – it was called Parksfield then. The victim survived but suffered burns. There were two women involved. The charge was GBH, dropped in favour of ABH after two witnesses for the prosecution changed their stories, and the victim's injuries – although severe burns – weren't actually classified as life-changing. The boy made a full recovery.

Jones escaped prison with a period of community service. Once you've got a hearing which resulted in a conviction, you've got access to court records as well as police. The magistrate's summing up is insightful on Jones's character. It would seem (and I'm kind of quoting here) that Jones is a Svengali-type personality. A need to dominate and control – particularly women, of whom he kept a small circle. Two of the women also with cannabis possession convictions and suspended sentences are named, but because in their case no violence was involved, there's no further details. One of them was Stacey Albarn… now, where have I heard that name before?'

Oooh, ouch, Chas! I just didn't think he'd pursue it. I'm staggered – sarcastic as well. This is a side to Chas I didn't expect.

There's a long pause. Chas is *not* going to say the second woman's name and, you know, I'm damned if I'm going to say anything either!

There's another even longer pause. Chas is looking out of the window, up the garden, and it's me that's looking at him.

'Cha-as?'

He turns to look at me but still doesn't speak.

'Chas. Would you do something for me?'

'What… you blaggin' me 'ead.' It's not quite a question; it sounds more like leftover words that just fell out of his mouth.

'I have to go back to Golightly. I need closure. I'd like you to drive me there. Would you do that?'

'When?'

'Soon, before the summer season ends.'

Suddenly, we're both laughing. It's neither joy nor amusement, and quite possibly completely unexplainable.

20

'Early start?'

'Fine.' It was something we were both used to. Him with his Wetlands and me with what had been sometimes ridiculous travel schedules.

'According to Google, from Springhurst Hill to Golightly takes three hours and fifty-three minutes.'

'Seven o'clock start then?'

I'd guessed we wouldn't need more than three hours at the house, so, start back at between two and three. It was late August so at least we'd be back in daylight. We'd looked at B&Bs; there were also cottages and houses – self-catering – but since my disaster I'd felt an unexpected reluctance to be away even for one night. But "away" from what? For the last four months I'd been a kind of bird perching, sooner or later I had to fly on. I'd looked at properties – online only, of course. Houses, flats, nothing inspired. Matching Thorpe was unique, so I'd just have to change my attitude; events had changed me. Chas had even joked, 'Downsizing? Lorna, you've achieved the ultimate in downsizing!' It was true and I'd lost everything – except the cabriolet, which Chas would be driving today. One thing was certain: the two of us wouldn't be sharing a property permanently – we were both equally agreed on that. Most couples would have spent a lot of time discussing that, but we're not most couples. The other point was that most couples might even discuss the matter with friends or relatives, but we don't have many – or any – of those. There's Matt, of course, but he's "got his own life", as they say. As for Chas, it's always been a bit of a mystery, but then that's what attracted me to him in the first place. It was like going out with a clean slate. The weird thing was that although Chas had finished the teaching, he was earning from the local paper, so between the two of us he was the breadwinner. Even though I didn't need the money, him earning and me not, now that was something I didn't like.

*

The police hadn't been to see me again; in fact, it had all gone quiet on the Golightly front. On the other matter, I'd got my bank cards back and Chas's pendant – minus its chain. The boy was pathetic, and I even felt sorry for him. He made me a formal face-to-face apology, accompanied by a policewoman – sincere, I thought – and an out-of-court settlement for the jewellery chain and bag, which had been hardly Gucci, more charity shop, if I recall. I said I didn't want to make any criminal charges against the boy, just a police warning. Chas thought it was a good result. He'd shown amazing restraint at the scene. Most men would have gone berserk seeing their partner mugged.

That DS emailed me – the laptop had gone, I'd been using my phone for emails, but I was amazed at the speed at which "Lee the computer" (Chas's local man) sorted me out and got me back into the world of e-commerce. The DS still couldn't confirm whether there'd be an inquest or not, but the feeling was that there probably wouldn't be unless somebody turned up with something outstanding. Evidently, the family were satisfied with the result of the post-mortem. As there were "no suspicious circumstances", the coroner released the body for cremation after only a short delay. What annoyed me was the press. It was all about how big the sinkhole story was, but how insignificant the coverage had been on Stacey's death. Local press, that's as far as it seemed to go! Only appearing on the newsfeeds of interested local folk: "*Emergency services were called to Golightly when a woman entered the reservoir…*" (I loved that word, "entered"), "*the woman was later confirmed to have suffered a fatal heart attack and the relatives have been informed.*" No name, no mention of a witness – thank God – and not a whisper of the fact that for the last few days of her life people thought she was called Diane Viggiano, and not until she was dead did they know she was Stacey Albarn. But I knew of someone who would be relieved that an inquest looked unlikely: Mr "Fuck-Brain" Jones, who, as front-of-house manager on the night of the fatal incident, could well have been requested to appear at the inquest to give account of himself. How well-oiled were the wheels of the Golightly publicity machine, and how fortunate to have friends in high places!

'It's the A1 – pretty much all the way.'

Chas said this with some glee. When he had to drive any distance – longitudinally, that was – it was always the A1, whereas I preferred the M1; it was quicker and you didn't have to keep slowing for roundabouts. Chas was also a fan of Little Chefs, and it was a sad day for him in 2018 when they became defunct. The Burger Kings and Costa Coffees which replaced them were no substitutes for Chas. Chas's opinion is that Britain is declining into something which is "route-dependent" rather than "a celebration of place". 'Everything's been virtualised,' he says. 'You can travel anywhere in your head on Google Street Scene, but wherever it is it's nearly all on the roads. The whole country has become one bloody great schematic diagram. It puts all the power in the hands of those who deal the motor car, those who fix it, and those who fuel it.' He only learnt to drive when he met me.

You know that phrase "The world owes me a living"? Chas hates it, thinks it's just for social parasites. The gospel according to Chas is that every one of us has a debt to pay to the world, because for the last three hundred years everybody – that is, in the developed world – has been enjoying the benefits of steam power, oil, gas, electricity, and never once have we paid back the earth's resources that we've been taking. And that includes what Chas calls "the armchair-bound *Guardian*-reading uni-educated – and largely salaried by courtesy of the British taxpayer – elite". He says, 'It's a bank account, only it's labelled "earth's resources" and we've been borrowing from it to fund something called "growth" and never paying back a fucking brass razoo.' Chas only swears when he gets passionate. He just won't accept those talking heads, some of whom have PhDs, who try to mitigate by claiming that scientists in the eighteenth century didn't understand the concept of earth's resources not being infinite. 'Of course they effing-well did! If the third president of the United States, Thomas Jefferson, could go out and buy a meteorological kit and prove to himself that all the stuff that was being pumped out of chimneys into the atmosphere was heating up the earth, then so could members of the Royal Society. And for the simple reason that it's not even science, it's home economics. It's the Mr Micawber principle: *annual income £20, annual expenditure; £19,19 shillings and sixpence, happiness. Annual income £20, annual expenditure; £20, 0 shillings and sixpence, misery!*'

Chas says that rising energy costs are long overdue; they're the result of energy companies failing to reinvest profits in green energy - as they were advised to by scientists after World War 2 – but because it was so expensive they decided to just maximise their customers. 'Now we're at two minutes to midnight and they're being forced to reinvest in green energy – which, of course, is still at a premium because nobody went against the grain and actually invested in it. So now we have to pay the price, Lorna. The era of cheap chickens is over.'

Peterborough, Grantham, and Newark. The blue or green signs loomed, then passed. We hardly spoke, even when we took a services break. It didn't matter, the talk we'd had after Chas's little detective work, had cleared some air between us. More to the point, it focussed on the reason I'd asked for the trip in the first place. I'd wanted some kind of revenge on Nick Jones. I knew I wasn't going to get it, but whatever happened, I wanted to involve Chas, let him into the strangeness of the whole thing. When we'd been sitting in his kitchen at Springhurst Hill after his revelations about Jones and Albarn, we'd laughed. Me out of relief, I suppose; him? Well, Chas had been dying for an opportunity to see Golightly. It was too late to expect a sighting of the Willow Warbler, but there was always the chance of him encountering a cluster of Golightly mushroom. Edible? Not a hope! Totally indigestible and sometimes – as we now knew – fatal.

21

'What time is it?'

Signs were saying Pontefract & Castleford, so I knew we were in the North. We'd just had a toilet stop but now Chas had left the A1 and we were sitting in a near-stationary line of local traffic – vans and trucks which appeared to have been diverted by road closures.

'Twenty to ten, I thought we'd break for coffee.'

'Thanks, Chas.'

I was aware that Chas was very particular about his coffee, hated Costa Coffee and all those high street commercial offers, so we'd brought a thermos. He'd pulled away from the diverted traffic into a lay-by where he brought the car to stop. But the scene was desolate, and uncannily like the lay-by where he had stopped near Harlow when he had broken the news to me about my house. Chas looked at his watch again while I poured the coffee. He would never drive on the motorway with the roof down, nor would he ever open the car window, but as we were to be drinking coffee, he had allowed himself the luxury of opening the windows so they wouldn't steam up.

'What do you see, Lorna?' This was the teacher coming out in him; he didn't do it often, thank goodness.

Over to my left and perhaps half a mile away were two very tall, thin-looking chimneys – perhaps hundreds of feet high – and behind them a massive, grey, lumpy, squarish building. Beyond and slightly over to the right were what looked like three fat cooling towers. Between them and us was a network of power pylons and cables. A grim sight, though a rather feeble sun enlivened the surface of the chimneys just enough to put me in mind of giant sticks of rather dull-coloured candy.

'Great place for coffee, Chas!' I looked at my coffee while, for the third time, Chas looked at his watch.

'Look at the chimneys, Lorna!'

I followed his instruction. As I took my first swallow of coffee, I was aware of movement at the base of each chimney. It looked as if the candy sticks were spitting out icing sugar and forming Saturn-type rings just above their bases. Slowly, almost imperceptibly at first, both chimneys leant to the right in perfect parallel, hung for a moment, apparently motionless, and then, as if in slow motion, noiselessly drifted to the earth. Simultaneously, the grey lump of a building became one vibrating wedge-shaped cloud of what looked like dust and smoke. There was a series of thuds which seemed to come from the road itself under the car, light thuds considering the vast building mass which had just been displaced before our eyes. The dust cloud rose, grew, spread and tumbled towards us. For a moment I thought it would reach us and envelope us like one of those terrible volcanic pyroclastic flows, but it stopped what must have been hundreds of yards away, suspended in the sultry air.

'Chas, you knew this was going to happen; why?'

He said nothing.

I could feel a succession of images surging through my mind like an unpleasantly swollen river; Christmas candles snapped at the base, upsetting archive film of executions by firing squad, the legs of the condemned crumpling at the knees. The legs of the two robbers crucified next to the supposedly dead Jesus being broken so that they would die more quickly due to suffocation. The body of Stacey plummeting down the spillway, and the dust cloud which must have risen in Matching Thorpe as my poor house slid underground. Yet I felt unaccountably calm; everything looked new, the landscape in front of us ready for change. We were just two people sitting in a car watching an historic event. It was cathartic; Chas must have been talking to the hype – '*Take her to a dramatic event, positive psychological shock.*'

'Thank you, Chas, it was amazing.'

'I'd read it was going to happen – 22nd August 2021 at 0945hrs. I thought we might just make it. It'll be on the news, and there'll be those YouTube films of it so you can watch it backwards.'

'Really?'

'Therapy reinforcement; it shows how nothing is permanent and how lots of things in life can be reversed.'

'Thank you for thinking of me.'

'Actually, Lorna, I desperately needed some new original copy for my nature column. I've been submitting old stuff for weeks. This is an historic step forward in the programme to achieve carbon neutrality by 2050. Next stop, Golightly!'

Chas could be very funny in a droll sort of way.

22

The magic was still working – the spell cast by the power station blow down, that is.

We were getting near Golightly. Chas left the highway and we were away from traffic fumes. One switch, the roof of the cabriolet slid open, and I could feel natural warmth at last. He drove along the road which pointed straight ahead and did not follow contours. Across land which had no fences, no hedges, and no dry-stone walls. We passed through the gatehouse in the yellow stone fake battlements, the stone soft-looking, *so* like lumps of candy that as the car slowed, I wanted to reach out and touch it, taste it, crazy! My intellect was telling me that I'd been here before – at least once – but my senses insisted that all was new. All I was certain of was that this time I felt unexpectedly happy.

There it was! The golden dome – still a good way away. Of *course*! Now I was a visitor – and incognito – we would not be driving right up to the house. The car park looked full so everything would be busy, but as I had not been here on a Sunday, nor in fact had I ever seen the car park before, I could not judge as to whether anything would be busy or not. Chas found a parking place next to the garden centre; one touch of the switch and the roof of the cabriolet wrapped itself closed, so silently. We slammed, so noisily. Chas locked and we walked hand in hand.

The visitors' entrance was in a low square building, two storeys, its centre hollowed out into a courtyard and paved with small stones which were uncomfortable to walk on. There was a café – indoor but with some tables outside where a few people were sitting drinking Coca-Cola and eating with their fingers. No face masks this time. There were toilets, what looked like an indoor exhibition space, and the ticket office. You had to walk through the ticket office to get into the house. There were lots of glass screens and those temporary barriers – metal posts with yards of retractable black canvas ribbon. Chas handed over the printouts of our tickets.

'Busy?' Feet tapping, knees bending slightly, Chas seemed to be in a hurry. Perhaps he was worried in case he missed seeing the shrill carder bee – or hearing it, whatever one did.

'Picking up, after covid.' The assistant was female, elderly, comfortable-looking. 'Most people come to walk in the grounds. A lot of folks just come for the garden centre. Eleven thirty for the twelve o'clock tour of the house, you're in good time.'

We'd booked – had to in the age of anno virus – the tour; why not? It could be interesting.

It took us a quarter of an hour to walk to the house, downhill and crunching past giant square-clipped hedges which screened rose gardens, until we emerged alongside a green dish of a lawn populated with colourfully dressed people sitting at widely spaced café tables. This time it seemed to be tea, coffee, and posh-looking biscuits. There was the odd salad here and there.

'Where are we?' I didn't recognise it.

'The west elevation.' Chas sounded slightly snappy. Our hands momentarily loosened their grip.

'Well, how should I know?' I giggled, perhaps nervously, and held Chas's hand just a little more firmly.

We went into the house via a modest-sized door. There was an A-board sitting on the paving which read *Visitor Entrance*. We showed our tickets at a glass screen, then I saw it, the oversized stone bust of Dionysus with the curly hair which looked like wriggling worms. I pulled Chas through the three feet of space between the bust and the stair balustrade.

'Look, Chas, this is the door we all piled out of after we got shut in the zodiac room!' I'd told him about that, it was a bit of harmless fun – but not about the message, that was too weird. He smiled, sniggered, and his head jerked back slightly. 'Where does the tour start?' I shouted back to the person who'd looked at our tickets – it was an annoyingly svelte and slinky female with lots of dark tumbledown hair and eyes with huge pupils.

'Here, but most of them are still sitting out in the sun.'

'Chas, we've just got time to see the front hall, before it gets full of people.' I'd had a sudden impulse. I pulled him behind me up the stone stair, across the wood block floor of the room with tall glass cabinets full of Etruscan vases, through a dark space with a low vaulted ceiling and into the gallery. The one with windows down one side and marble busts of Roman emperors lining the other. There were bars of light running across the floor and the whole corridor looked golden. The only movement was tiny dust motes I could see drifting from one side of the space to the other.

A figure appeared round the corner at the end of the gallery. As it stepped into one of the bars of light, I could see it was Spreighmont – Jones, that was. Same suit, same black Oxfords. He was strolling, dapper, perhaps on his way to deliver the tour. My hand slipped from Chas's, but before I could warn Chas, the man spoke.

'Lornaah!'

The emphasis on the last syllable made it sound like the kind of encouragement a husband might give his wife who had rashly agreed to take part in the mums' race at their daughter's sports day. He was beaming.

'How *are* you?'

He was standing like an oversized plaster statue of Christ (*so* concerned), the open arms of Jesus; how could he?

'And…' (turning), 'you must be Chas.'

He might just as well have also added in a throaty *lucky man!* He'd seen us holding hands. Over a four-month period it was unlikely to be anyone else. I felt trapped again, and the air around us seemed thick with misunderstanding.

'We were so sorry to lose you; it was an extremely unfortunate event, a tragedy. Are you here for the tour?'

Chas looked almost grateful for his – what seemed obvious to me bogus – concern. Surely not? The insincerity of the man! No indication of surprise that I might wish to return of my own volition to a location which was bound to be painful to me.

'Please excuse me, good to meet you, take good care.' He disappeared round the corner into the gloom, hurrying this time. I felt a sudden desolate chill.

'So *that's* him?' Chas said it with a "What's all the fuss about?" air, and – I couldn't help feeling – not without a touch of… could it be jealousy?

'Chas? Would you mind awfully if we didn't go on the tour?'

He didn't seem exactly disappointed. 'Perhaps you'd prefer to walk up to the reservoir?'

'No, I need to sit down, after that.'

We went back to where all the tables were on the lawn; it was waitress service.

'Just a cup of tea.'

'Eat?'

'Later, maybe.'

I really didn't feel like a verdict from Chas on Jones. Not unless it was going to be pretty damning and in my favour. Slippery character? Underhand, untrustworthy, iffy? None of it. Chas was looking at me in a strange way – not head on, just glancing. Why? He had the facts, he'd done the digging, but there was something else going on with Chas. Just what had I told Chas about Jones? Nothing. That was the trouble, that was the root of it, the essence of everything: I'd concealed.

I could see a woman staring at me, three tables away. There were two people, a man and a woman, sitting at a table set for four. I knew her, but it took a few moments before it permeated my shocked brain. It was that damned medium, but I couldn't remember her name.

'Look, I've just seen somebody who was on the course. I'll have to go and say hello.'

'What, face like a robber's dog?'

'Ch-as!' I almost slapped him. Then I thought he looked relieved, as if he needed a least a few seconds alone to compose himself. I got up, left him with his mineral water and salad, and walked across towards the couple.

'Lorna!' Her forehead puckered slightly, voice

breathy but sympathetic this time, I could feel it. 'Trish! Trish Westfall… and this is Rob.'

How could I forget? Small of stature with a furrowing brow and the large worried eyes of a dachshund, and that mouth – oh God, when it was open and moaning!

'That's Chas.' I was pointing over my shoulder. 'Trish, would you mind awfully if we came and joined you for a few minutes? I'd invite you over to us, but we've only got a table for two.' I had to diffuse the tension with Chas. I beckoned.

Chas got up, bottle of mineral water in one hand and still munching on sun-dried tomatoes. We sat down.

'Maybe we should tell the waitress you've moved tables. She'll think you've done a runner.'

'Ro-ob!'

'Well, from what I hear, nobody could do a runner from here.' Chas seemed to have come out of his state of "monk on".

'*I* managed it!'

Everybody laughed, and thank *God*!

'Yes, but you'd paid in advance and you didn't get your money back… So, what brought *you* back here today?' Chas was looking at Trish.

'Sorry about Chas. He can't help asking direct questions, it's the journalist in him.'

'Journalism, really?' Rob sounded interested.

'Just a nature column for the local paper. No crime.'

'So, out of the four of us, I'm the only non-writer here.'

'In what way?'

'I'm a seismologist.'

'Christ!'

'Cha-as!'

'Well, you know there's a sinkhole opened up at Matching Thorpe?'

'That's not characteristic karst terrain.'

Chas looked fascinated, mouthed a "What?".

Rob replied, 'I'd seen it on the news.'

'Well, Lorna's troubles weren't over when she left here.'

'That was *you*?' Trish sounded mortified. She looked more like a dachshund than ever. 'Lorna, I'm so sorry, it said on the news that everything was lost.'

'It's okay, the insurance money is on its way, I'm looking at properties. Meanwhile, I'm driving Chas up the wall at his place. But yes, it's not like having your car stolen, it's start again, but I'm looking at life in a new way. It has to have its good points.'

'But you still haven't answered my question.'

'Don't be so rude, Chas!'

'He's right to be curious. Two reasons, I suppose; I'd really enjoyed the course and wanted to show Rob, but point two, there were a few things I felt uneasy about.'

'With the management?'

'That, and the house in general.'

'Trish told me about the séance.'

I hoped she hadn't told him about the message. There was something intensely personal merely about the idea of that, even if I hadn't been able to make head nor tail of it.

'To tell you the truth, I was surprised – at the way everybody dealt with it.'

'The spooks?'

'The way everybody took it so seriously. I mean, as I said, I'm not a qualified medium, I just went on a course.'

'People do, most people – even if they scoff, they have some degree of respect, and we all have our fears.' Please don't let her mention the message now!

'The thing that worried me was the way we were locked in. It was deliberate and it was extreme. People don't pay to be scared like that. I wanted to show the zodiac room to Rob.'

'And did you?'

'As you know, Lorna, that section of the house is off limits to the public.'

'… And?'

'We had to dodge under one of those red ropes.'

'Unsurprisingly – according to Trish – the zodiac room was locked today, but there's no doubt that you being locked in was deliberate because those corridors are all covered on CCTV. "They", or he or she, saw you going in.'

'So, *you'll* have been observed today?'

'We went on the eleven o'clock tour, stuck with the group, hung back and wandered off to look at the room. After we've enjoyed meeting you, we're going, so we don't really care.'

'Did you see anything of the management when you were on your tour?'

'Just that one with the moustache; I think he recognised me but he didn't give any sign of acknowledgement. What about you?'

'Ohhh yeees! He came and said his hello. Very corporate!' I was looking at Chas for indications of which side of the fence he might now be sitting. He was looking at Rob, impressed no doubt by his credentials as a seismologist. 'I wouldn't worry about his not saying hello, Trish. Not many students attract the kind of attention I managed!' I thought I could detect a "Don't blame yourself for what happened" expression on Trish's face.

'He did pick on you, Lorna, right from the start.'

'Thank you, Trish,' I said. I could see Chas's eyebrows raising a millimetre.

'Talk of the devil.' Rob was looking straight past my right shoulder. 'Who's the other guy?'

I turned to see two male figures standing outside the visitors' door by the A-board. The one with his back to me was Jones, the one facing our way and every few seconds – or was I imagining it? – glancing at me, was Golightly. It was as if they were there for our – or even perhaps just my – benefit.

'The eponymous Golightly.'

Perhaps Golightly had heard Trish. I hadn't moved, I was still staring at the back of Jones's head, as if throwing darts of hate at it. The two figures began to walk away, up a flight of stone steps, Jones cantering ahead slightly. Just before they disappeared round the corner and along the north elevation, Jones turned, looked straight at me, and – was I going mad, again? – winked. In a completely different scenario, it might well have been a blink, a twitch, a stroboscopic effect of the sun. I couldn't be sure.

'Lorna, he winked at you!' Rob obviously didn't know whether to laugh.

'*He did.*' Trish's voice was one of sober affirmation.

'Fuck him!' I stood up, tried to take a step in the direction of the vanishing men, but Chas had me by the arm. 'You saw it, Chas!'

'I missed it actually. Anyway, Lorna, you *were* staring at them.'

I couldn't believe it. That, and Chas's reaction. It was an appalling display – particularly considering the shock of what happened at the reservoir. *So* flippant! I was, however, determined not to make any more of a scene than I'd already done. Several heads at neighbouring tables had turned.

'We have to go, Chas. If you'll just excuse me.' I made for the ladies' room with Rob's voice just audible.

'These guys are playing games; they're just frustrated failed actors, and they treat everybody here as a captive audience. The trouble with actors is you don't know when they're acting and when they're not. There's nothing anybody can do.'

As I rounded the corner out of earshot, I found myself agreeing with what Rob had just said. Not only had I been a drama student, in many covert ways I had been acting since the age of fifteen. But had Rob known what Chas and I knew – and what I hadn't told

Chas – Rob might have taken a different view. But I had a horrible feeling that he was right, and that's how things were going to stay. But Chas, *Chas*! He was being all grown up, absurdly open-minded and "We mustn't start a witch hunt" type of thinking. But how could I tell him the rest of the story, and would it make any difference anyway?

Staring at my still-enraged face in the ladies' room mirror, I saw another figure appear behind me.

'Lorna, did you manage to look at that message?'

I was so wound up that, at first, I hadn't a clue what she was talking about.

'Have you still got the napkin with Boone's numbers?'

I had, and I felt a wave of shame wash over me because in spite of the fact that I'd found nothing in it to make sense, I'd kept it, right there in my bag. It was creepy. On the one hand, I'd wanted nothing to do with it; on the other, it seemed like a link with a world that I did not understand, a psychic universe of which I, like many millions of others, was in denial of, but knew damn well contained things which were ineluctably part of us. It was a touchstone. When I started speaking, my intention was to say, 'No and I've lost it,' but something intangible was floating behind my shoulder.

'Actually, Trish... I've got it here, but it didn't seem to make any sense. I think it... I mean the spirit, may have been mistaken.'

'May I have a look?'

I'd put it in an old compact to keep it safe – ridiculous, as if it were a precious object, a photo of a loved one instead of a grubby napkin folded however many times. I opened the compact, held it up and blew away the surplus powder.

'I worked through it and put the letters against Boone's numbers but couldn't see anything in it. It doesn't look like Latin…'

Trish took the paper from me, studied it for a moment, then reached in her bag, took out a pen and a pad of Post-it notes – the pale blue ones.

'It's written in reverse. They often do that – or Boone might simply have noted it down like that.'

I was hit by a sudden gust of fury. To miss something so overwhelmingly obvious. But as I saw what she was spelling out under the letters I'd written, I felt a chill across my stomach.

A – N – R – O – L – U – O – Y – E – V – I –
G – R – O – F – I
I FORGIVE YOU LORNA

'Lorna, this was an unborn spirit. I sensed that when it first came to us because it felt so light and bright it almost sparkled.'

'Do the unborn have spirits?' I was blurting defensively, but Trish was on top of her game.

'According to some texts, Jesus Christ was unborn.'

The chill travelled down deep into my pelvis and seemed to settle somewhere in my lower back. At the same time, I could feel a violent hot flush to the top of my head, sinking to my forehead, then plunging to my neck and chest. I was breathing heavily and I could hear an awful braying noise. I could see a mouth in the mirror – my mouth, gaping. All of a sudden, my face was streaming wet and I was panting, fighting for air which didn't seem to exist. I could feel the other person in the room holding my wrists.

As I began to calm, I was conscious of the rushing of water, followed by a sharp tap, then a deep thud. The blurred image of a figure emerged from one of the cubicles.

'Are you all *roight,* moi luvvly?'

'I will be.' I was still gasping, still trying to stem the flood of forty years of guilt feelings.

'She's just had a shock – a good kind of shock.'

'Oi can get you a chur if you loik.'

'That's very kind of you.'

Seconds later, I was seated. Trish was speaking, very slowly.

'Lorna, does the name Ainsworth mean anything to you?'

'I don't think so.'

Trish held up another Post-it note.

H – T – R – O – W – S – N – I – A
AINSWORTH

'No.' I felt my head shaking.

'This is the one I'm not happy about. This spirit did

not go to the Light. There's no message as such, it's as if it's merely announced its presence. It's angry, Lorna. I sensed that it's an old spirit, at least three hundred years. I felt it may be connected with the house, but that doesn't mean to say it can't travel elsewhere… Lorna, are you feeling better?'

'Yes, thank you.'

I was, my mind was racing, and the more Trish was talking, the more I was realising that I had not told her the truth. '*Connected with the house.*' *The Building of Golightly.* The name was in there, I was sure, but I would have to check when I got back to Springhurst Hill.

'Lorna, this spirit may have attached itself to you. There's something called spirit release. You can get treatment for it.'

'Really?' Like mortgage release? I was aghast.

'There're several ways; there's religious exorcism, but that's used less frequently these days. Also, it's not sufficient just to get rid of a spirit, it has to go to the Light. Hypnotherapy is the modern method of choice… Lorna, do you understand? You need to think carefully about this.'

'I am doing. Please go on.'

'You have to consult a hypnotherapist, they'll either put you into an altered state – hypnosis, that is – and communicate with the spirit through you, or the therapist will have psychic powers in which case they'll be able to work directly with the spirit.'

'How?'

She either misunderstood or ignored me.

'It's not available on the NHS…'

I was giggling, the thought of it.

'You have to go privately; contact the Royal College of Psychiatrists, they'll advise you.'

'You think I'm still mentally ill?'

'I didn't say that. I think you may have something called spirit attachment.'

'Thank you, Trish.' All at once I was standing, hugging her. 'Look, we have to go.'

'The men will be wondering what's happened.'

'They'll probably be talking about the seismology of journalism. My face tells a story, they'll just have to be discreet.'

'We thought you'd fallen down the plughole.'

'Thanks, Chas. I just felt a bit faint, and a nice lady from Norfolk got me a chair to sit on.'

'Lorna, since you missed the end of the course, have you thought about putting all these events down on paper, writing a novel about it?'

'I've done more than think about it, Trish. I've done it – at least it's nearly complete, I just don't know how to finish it.'

Oooh, look at Chas's face!

'*I* didn't know anything about this, Lorna!'

'What did you think I was doing while you were writing your nature column?'

And Trish, there's more than a touch of envy there. I'd say she was downright jealous.

'Where are you parked?'

'Near the garden centre.'

'We're there as well; we'll walk over with you.'

'Keep in touch, Lorna, let me know how you are.'

'It's almost two o'clock. Chas, you didn't get your walk up to the reservoir.'

'We're coming back, aren't we?'

'I've a strange feeling we may well be or, at least, I may *need* to.'

We're hugging and shaking hands. When I saw Trish two hours ago, I couldn't even remember her name and I couldn't have given a damn about her. Now I see that whatever I think about her, the two of us are inextricably bound together by one piece of intensely personal knowledge. Chas unlocks the cabriolet, gets in, opens the hood. Trish and Rob walk to their car. It's a Fiat 500, in one of those limp retro pastel shades, pistachio or something. She's driving.

23

'Thank God for that. I thought we were never going to get away.'

'So, *that's* the famous Lorna!'

'She was always stirring things up, right from the start… Oh Lord, she's coming back; sorry to let this heat in, Rob, I'll have to put the window down to see what she wants now.'

Lorna's bending forward, her hand extended as if she wants to touch Trish. She straightens up, the hand pulls away as if she's thought better of it.

'Trish, do you believe in automatic writing?'

There's an uncomprehending pause. Trish fails to hide the sigh she's feeling and exhales wearily.

'It's not whether I *believe* in it, Lorna. What I think – or anybody else, for that matter – is irrelevant. It just is… it exists.'

'I only wondered.' She shrugs, apparently doesn't want to say any more.

'Bye!'

'Take care.'

'Oh dear! Oh dear!! Oh dear!!! She *really* is in trouble, and there's absolutely nothing more I can do to help her.'

24

Hello, Chas – Phil, I should say.

Since we ran into one another I've been thinking. I wonder if you might do me a little favour, in return. You see I've applied for this job – a teaching job – and I know you're a teacher now, and I need a reference. You'd be perfect, Phil, because you came up the hard way and your word will go a long way. I need this job very badly, because like you, Phil, my life needs to change.

How's Lorna by the way?

Your old mate, Reuben

It's exactly the same as his previous email, except he's added two words, "*in return*", implying he did me a favour. He did not! He's just jealous of someone who's made something of his life against all odds. So clever! Designed to go unnoticed to all unlikely readers of this mail – except me. Oh, and now Lorna. Christ!

LORNA'S POSTSCRIPT

This is when it happens, when *Tubular Bells* is on. No, I don't mean the Van Dyk brothers and their awful dinging and bonging. I mean the sublime and weird piece by Mike Oldfield. I've always loved it, since I was a child. It's gone midnight and I'm sitting at Chas's kitchen table, with my new PC; there's Chas's Anglepoise lamp and the hi-fi. I have this fancy that I can actually see the sound coming out of the speakers in waves of red and green.

> *Our Lorde was not alwayse frugally profuse in his designs. Much timber, if it be oak, is saved from older building to raise outer houses. Meulenbelt was sent to help me as I am not skilled in recording on payper.*
> *Ainsworth*

It's not hand*writing* of course. It's automatic *typing*. A spook may have been born and lived in an age of low tech, but if he or she has any self-respect they will know how to work a PC – except, of course, they're not, I am. They're working through me. Ainsworth is "illiterate", but remember, when the paranormal kicks in dyslexia can turn into a superpower. My fingers hit the keyboards and the spook tells me what to write. The uncanny thing is that I don't hear a voice telling me what to write; when I start typing, I don't know what's coming. The first I know of its meaning or form is when I see it appear on the screen.

> *Cornelissen instructed us in the digging and lining of drainnes. This involved ditches of a certainne depth. Some fifty or so persons were engaged. Some men were employed who hadde been dwelling in the twenty houses in the unpromising neighbourhood, but most had come from elleswhere.*
> *Ainsworth.*

What have I told Chas? The answer is very little. The professional guideline in my world was always "Only tell the client what he needs to know". You can apply the same rule to a domestic relationship. This coupledom pretence of "We have no secrets between us" is smugly unachievable. Human beings can't do anything without generating secrets. It's hunting survival, it's instinct.

> *The twenty or so dwellings had to be demolished, so cleared of tenants. Some were agreeable to take employment either in raising ye grrt pile, or on ye newwe estate. Others dispersed to neighbouring*

settlements. One family made known to Meulenbelt that they shalle not leave even if the house be burnned around them.
Ainsworth

I can't tell Chas about this even if I wanted to, because I would have to tell him about the message. I don't want to have to make up lies because I don't want Chas to know about my unborn child – it's too personal. Also, his knowing about this writing could jeopardise the future of my novel, the revelation of which Chas did not like and is no doubt on his mind at this very moment as he sits in his brown swivel chair writing up the events of the power station blowdown.

Much of the digging was done at nighte as Meulenbelt and I hadde been ordered by Cornelissen to work with grrt speed. Meulenbelt made it knowne to me that he had commanded ruffians to make flame to the walles and roof of the tenants' house. I came to the house and gave much effort to discourage the ruffians from their work in the knowledge that it was an inhumane act.
Ainsworth

We all have different personae, varying facets of the way we present ourselves to the world. Convenient categories might be: professional, home, relatives, leisure interests. Of course, that's crude trying to compartmentalise – there will be lots of subtle overlaps.

Nevertheless, each of us is like a pie chart; X will claim to "know" a certain size slice of that pie, Y another, Z a different size and so forth. There's some sense in that, but where it all starts to go wrong is in human time spans, insofar as a person who is a relative will invariably miscalculate the size of their slice of the pie because they have known the subject "since they were *that* high". They think it's all about length of time, whereas it's really all about intensity of relationship or experience. So where *is* the "true" you?

I'm frightened of Ainsworth. He's a bit like a dangerous pet, but he's *mine, mine*! And I'm determined to keep him. I couldn't give him up if I tried for the very simple reason that he is the only contact I have with my unborn child. My only link. I can't give him up, I can't! He could bite me, but I'm drawn by the danger; it's stimulating, inspiring, and I've got my book to think about now, that's my baby, my *only* baby. Ainsworth will decide how it ends.

> *My efforts were in vain and the heat from the fyre was so greate that all present hadde to drawe back. The noise of cracking tymbres and the screams of those inside so fearful that manye of the ruffyans fled. Meulenbelt ordered water to be fetched so that the bodies of the burned wretches within coulde be brought forth; a man, a woman, and a newborne infant, blackened and ungodly.*
> *Ainsworth*

Matt has never shown any interest in who his father is. Sooner or later, this will change, and he will want to know. Chas will now have assumed that Jones is Matt's father and this I can confirm, but there's much more to it than that. What no one will ever question is who Matt's mother is. Throughout my life, not only have I concealed information from others, I have been shamelessly dishonest with myself, and Matt, but I had little alternative. Until Matt was eight, he believed I was his sister, and Mum and Dad encouraged that. It was convenient; it made sense and meant that I could go off and have a college life and career while my parents did all the work bringing Matt up. But the events of the past few months have uncovered a need in me to come out of denial and admit to myself that in spite of all I have said, Matt is *not* my child.

So much had I wanted the unborn child – whose spirit came to me in the zodiac room at Golightly – that I stole Matt from his real mother, my mother. When I say stole, I didn't do it literally of course. I did it by perpetuating the myth which my contemporaries already believed, in that they assumed that Matt was my child. They assumed that it had been me that had become pregnant and that it had been a family decision that my parents would take on the role of bringing Matt up while I went to college. It was easy, it was a myth which other people had created for me, all I had to do was to go along with it. The truth is somewhat different. Jones stayed at our house several times, and Mum took a shine to him. She succumbed to his charisma, as I had done. Though some might have thought my mother was "a little old" for conceiving a second child, there was never any suspicion because Dad always assumed Matt was his. Whyever not? It never felt as if I was even deceiving me, as the years went by I really and truly came to believe it myself.

When he's ready I *will* tell Matt about Jones, but I cannot tell him about Mum. Even a DNA test wouldn't reveal the truth. Meanwhile, I have to come to terms with the fact that I have lied to myself for thirty-six years and that really and truly I am childless. By pretending I was a single parent, I believed that I gave myself status, wisdom, experience. Without a child I feel no more than a child myself. Whether I ever make this known to Chas or not I am undecided.

Meulenbelt ordered that we hide the bodies of the man, woman and child – which I believe was a boy – in the drainnes trench. I took on a fearful protest during which I layed handes on Meulenbelt and the two ruffians who dragged the bodies into the trench. Two further ruffians came at me from behynde and struck me with stout oak beams across my neck and then with stones to my heade. The four of us are still buried under the lake, north east of the Temple of the Four Wyndes.
Ainsworth

AND AT 1100 HRS THE NEXT MORNING

Boy, 11, pleads not guilty to murder of boy, 5.
The Birkenhead Gazette, 1983

It was in the national papers as well. Due to the seriousness of the crime, Crown Court, case lasted several days, verdict of manslaughter and the sentence: "To be detained at her Majesty's pleasure". Anonymity was lifted and the name of the killer revealed.

I was only one year old when the case of Mary Bell was in the papers, and too young to remember the Moors Murderers, but when the story of Jamie Bulger's murder broke in 1993, I was a young woman of twenty-seven and not too wrapped up with the Paco Rabanne account to not have had that name ringing in my ears for several weeks as I made my daily journey to work. Ten years prior to that I'd been still at school, rarely watched or listened to the news, and was an infrequent reader of newspapers, so the case of Lee Wardell, who was murdered in Birkenhead Merseyside after being "*abducted by two boys*" totally failed to register on my teenage radar. Though two boys had been involved in the abduction, the second – according to reports – argued with the killer, told him to leave the victim alone and then left the scene. Only Philip Bradshaw was charged, taken to court – and according to various newspaper accounts which I have on the table in front of me – imprisoned and "*rehabilitated*" over a period of ten years before being released in a "*different part of the UK*" and issued with a new identity. Philip Bradshaw's childhood was part of – what we are nowadays, through extensive media reporting, led to believe is – a familiar pattern of the early lives of criminals: absentee father, mother worked as a prostitute, school truancy, and an apparent need for power and control over those around them – particularly their peers and those younger…

As I've already said, the name Philip Bradshaw was unknown to me until shortly after nine o'clock this morning, while Chas was out at a meeting with his newspaper bosses, when a taxi delivered a package which I opened with some caution as there is no indication who the sender is. With a little research, no doubt, I could find out… but right now I would rather not know. The parcel – a pale brown, or buff, you might say, jiffy bag – contains fifteen pages of A4, images photocopied and scanned from what appears from its pastel-coloured grainy leaves to be a painstakingly kept old scrapbook of newspaper cuttings. The sender has kindly printed the pages in colour and scanned them to a resolution of sufficient intensity to prove to me *beyond any reasonable doubt* that the person depicted – as a child of eleven years – in the various mug shots, is the same person as he who is my lover and has been a close part of my life for the past ten years. Charles (Chas) Peake and Philip Bradshaw are the same person.

Even if I were face blind, there are too many coincidences to ignore: timelines, a childhood which

Chas always said was bad and hinted was best forgotten. His frequent knack of lapsing into Merseyside twang. His admission that he got lucky by moving between swabbing floors and being a technical assistant to a handicraft teacher. By the time Chas actually started running the odd handicraft class because the school was desperate over staff absences, he would have been a familiar figure in his khaki-brown overall and mop bucket. *Well* before DBS checks and even before the CRB system came into force. Chas has often said, 'Woodwork made me!' He must have done it in prison; there was plenty of time for him to become proficient.

At least two of the newspaper reports make mention of a note found with the murdered child's body, though it was not proven that it had been written by Bradshaw. It reads, somewhat chillingly: *I kill so that I may come back*. The meaning is not clear. Was it simply childish grammar and should have read, *I kill* and *I may come back*, in the way of a threat that he might do it again? Or – given my brush with the supernatural over the last few months – did it mean something more spiritual in the vein of, *If I take a life, then that life belongs to me to put to my use in the future in the form of reincarnation*? Or even – anticipating some kind of reform process – *I do my worst act now, so that I may become better in future*? There were no doubt numerous slants one could put on the phrase. But Philip Bradshaw did not kill again, and there appears to be no evidence of any further violence, nor did he even offend again.

How do I feel? One small thing: the fact that this little stash of press cuttings is sitting right in front of me at all means that a blackmail attempt has failed. It's addressed to me, not Chas. He has refused to give in to blackmail, so good for him!

I will get over the shock of seeing a colleague – nay, *fellow convicted criminal* – collapse and die in front of me. I will accept that I will not get closure over Golightly, that I will receive no apology from bastard features Nick Jones for sexual harassment – thirty-six years after I allowed myself to be drawn into his web. I will recover from momentarily forgetting my name and losing my home and material possessions.

I now realise that I must give up Ainsworth. He's not mine to keep, so I *will* contact the Royal College of Psychiatrists, do what I can to help Ainsworth towards the Light, and will inform the police that there may be three adults and a child buried under the lake near the temple of the Four Winds at Golightly. I understand that for some years police have been engaging psychics to help with certain investigations, and though time will have ensured that *this* case will be archaeological and anthropological rather than a police forensic matter, perhaps what is sometimes referred to as a "decent burial" may be possible.

Coming to terms with the fact that for the last ten years I have been living closely with a convicted child killer may never happen. How could I have missed it? At least the fact that I'd been living with someone who'd committed a crime so serious as to be considered "beyond the pale". There have always been sufficient clues, but I just never saw them. No, that's not correct; I saw them, but I didn't hold them in the right light. In a way, the closer we come to someone, the less we really know them. It's all relative and, yes, Chas is right when he says we're all in denial, about many things.

All this doesn't mean that Chas and I may abruptly desert one another, or drift apart. Unless the attempted blackmailer makes another move, not a word may be said between Chas and I about this. Philip Bradshaw was *"released in 1993 as being considered as posing no threat to the public."* Bradshaw wasn't just "rehabilitated" and given a fresh identity. That's not sufficient for anybody! He was given a *choice*; of either continuing with the mindset of Philip, or attempting to redevelop his personality as Chas, and over the time I've known him, he's done that. Chas and Philip may be the same biological body, but Chas is no longer Philip. Chas ceased being Philip thirty years ago, so it's unthinkable that the two of us might ever discuss the matter.

I may be so, so wrong, but faced with such a situation all I can do is to reach into my innermost self and put all trust in intuition. Some crimes are crimes of such enormity that they defy intellectual appraisal, are bigger than an individual… *Was it due to reasons of the defendant's genetic personality or environment?* They can only belong to humanity and are therefore a challenge to the very soul of Man.

There is no doubt that if Philip Bradshaw had killed *my* child, my only child – had the child that I allowed to be killed when it was unborn *become* a child – then I would have wanted Bradshaw punished, perhaps even wished him dead. But that's not the point, because since I was nineteen, I've firmly believed that no one is beyond redemption. Of course, whether they can develop into it or not is another matter. Punishment embitters all, those who receive it and they who are charged with the task of meting it out.

"Rehabilitation", as they call it, is the only way, and it's working, it's been working for ten, twenty, thirty years. But rehabilitation doesn't stop at the point of release, or even later, it never stops, it's for life, it *has* to be, and I'm part of that life now, for better or for worse. Chas and I will do it together.

It is not now as it hath been of yore: -
Turn wheresoe'er I may,
By night or day,
The things which I have seen I now can see no more.

Intimations of Immortality from Recollections
of Early Childhood
William Wordsworth

ENDNOTES

i   Actually, the figure appears to be an underestimate. According to https://explodingtopics.com/blog/smartphone-stats it's more like 7 billion mobile phone owners and 17 billion devices.

ii Peter Frankopan, statement made 'in conversation' event The Earth Transformed, held at St Peter's School at York Literature Festival, March 2023.

This book is printed on paper from sustainable sources managed under the Forest Stewardship Council (FSC) scheme.

It has been printed in the UK to reduce transportation miles and their impact upon the environment.

For every new title that Troubador publishes, we plant a tree to offset CO_2, partnering with the More Trees scheme.

For more about how Troubador offsets its environmental impact, see www.troubador.co.uk/sustainability-and-community